DELLA'S DESPERATION

ELLA CORNISH

CHAPTER 1

*D*ella Gordon peered through the spindles of the staircase in the hallway, watching as her father opened the door. While she should have been abed hours ago, Della found it difficult to sleep when she knew that her parents were out, wanting to see her mother's beautiful dress once more. It was a lovely dress, one that she had longed to reach out and touch to see if the material was as soft as it looked when they had come to kiss her goodnight.

Of course, she didn't dare. Her mother didn't like Della wrinkling her skirts when they were going out for the evening, though her father had allowed her to throw her arms around his legs and hug him lovingly. Her mother had scolded Della for doing so, but her father had just chuckled and ruffled her hair before handing her back over to her nanny.

Now they were home, and Della was hoping that they would discuss the performance that they had just seen.

Before her father could remove his evening coat, there was a knock on the door, startling the couple. Della watched as he slowly opened the door again.

"What is the meaning of this?" he asked as three men wearing overcoats moved into the darkened hallway. "I say, do you know what time of night it is?"

"Mr Thomas Gordon," one of them stated, his thick moustache rending Della of a caterpillar she had once found in the small garden at the rear of the house, "you are being arrested."

Her mother gasped; her hands frozen on the wrap she had been removing. "Arrested? Thomas? What is the meaning of this?"

"This has to be some sort of mistake," Della heard her father state. "On what grounds?"

One of the men laid a hand on her father's shoulder, his expression sympathetic. "It's over, Thomas. Your creditors have come calling and they aren't going to let you run yourself into debt any longer."

"Thomas?" Della heard her mother ask, her voice nothing more than a squeak. "Whatever are they talking about?"

Della expected her father to explain that they had the wrong home but instead he slumped his shoulders and she nearly gasped aloud at the glimmer of tears she saw in his eyes. Her father never cried, never, and Della knew then that something was amiss, very amiss.

"Iona, my love," he said softly, reaching out to grasp her hand in his. "I'm sorry."

Della's mother's lips parted. "What did you do, Thomas?"

The other men shuffled their feet as her father moved to stand in front of her mother, drawing her against him. "I wanted to take care of you and Della. But my position as clerk couldn't afford this, this lifestyle."

Della didn't know what work her father truly did when he left their home every day, but he always carried a briefcase with him and when he came home in the evenings, his fingers were stained with ink. She also didn't know what a lifestyle was, but it was clear to her that it had something to do with her mother's dress by the way she was looking at it.

"Mr Gordon," one of the men stated, clearing his throat, "you and your family will need to come with us."

"N...no," her father stated, his eyes widening. "Not my family. They can stay here while I sort this out."

The man shook his head. "There's nothing to be sorted. Your presence is requested at King's Bench, immediately."

Her mother's sharp intake of breath made Della wrinkle her nose. Whatever King's Bench was, her mother didn't want to go.

Della decided she didn't either.

"Please," her father was begging now as her mother started to cry softly. "Please don't subject them to this. It is my fault, and I will pay for my crime, but they are innocent. My daughter..."

"I'm sorry," the man replied, glancing at her mother. "I will allow you some time to gather your belongings but be quick about it. You are a fine man,

Thomas, and will be treated as such as long as you come with us now."

Della waited with bated breath to hear her father say anything that would mean they could stay in their home, but he just nodded, and she rushed to her room, tears blinding her eyes. They were going to have to leave her home. She didn't want to leave her home!

Hurrying into her room, Della climbed into bed quickly and pulled the covers over her, turning on her side to face the window instead of the door. If she hurried, she could go to sleep before her father came in and this would all be a dream. He would laugh and kiss her cheek, telling her to go back to bed and when she woke, there would be no men in the hallway wanting to take them away.

When Della finally heard footfalls in her room, it wasn't her father's. The room brightened and her mother was shaking her shoulder, forcing her daughter to look at her.

"Wake up," her mother stated, her voice raw. "Della!"

Della turned and met her mother's reddened eyes. "Mama?" she asked, hoping that her voice was sleepy enough. "What's wrong?"

"Marcie," her mother said instead, addressing the nanny that hovered close by the bed, her face streaked with tears. "Gather her things. She will need warm clothing, the warmest you can find. Leave anything that won't fit into the suitcase. She can only take one bag."

Della pushed herself to a seated position. "I don't want to leave. It is the middle of the night."

"Hush now," her mother interrupted, her mouth tightening in displeasure. "Please, get out of the bed, Della. We don't have much time." Then she swept from the room and Marcie rushed forward, throwing the covers off Della. "Come now," she said in a gentle voice. "You mustn't make this any more difficult than it already is, Della. Help me pick out the things that you want to take."

Della did as she asked, choosing her favourite doll that her father had given her on her last birthday and a tea set in case she wished to play tea parties wherever they were going. Once she was dressed in her warmest stockings and dress, Della allowed Marcie to put on her coat and scarf, the one that had her mittens dangling from it. "Where am I going?" she asked her nanny, who wasn't dressed to travel with them.

Marcie's eyes filled with tears, and she hugged Della tightly. "Somewhere new, but only for a little while. I will see you before too long."

"All right," Della replied as her mother came to the doorway, dressed in her woollen coat. Della took her mother's hand and clutched her doll tightly in her grasp as they walked down the stairs to the hallway, where those men and her father waited. Her father looked worried, so Della didn't ask any sort of silly questions, remaining silent as they were loaded into the waiting hackney carriage.

The trip did not take long and when the door opened, Della found herself staring up at a large red building, the gas lights giving her only a glimpse of their destination.

"Mr Gordon," a man stated as Della stepped onto the sidewalk. "I have been waiting for ye."

His voice sounded a little funny to Della, as if he was talking with marbles in his mouth, but she didn't say anything, attempting to be as quiet as possible so that they could go back home quickly. She didn't like this place at all.

"Who might you be?" her father asked politely as Della's mother gathered her against her skirts.

"I'm Ron, Ron Fraser," the man answered. "I will be yer guide through this predicament ye have found yerself in."

Della decided that she couldn't stand to hold back her questions any longer. "What is wrong with your voice?" she asked.

"Della!" her mother gasped. "Apologise at once!"

The man waved his hand at her. "Nay, tis alright. I'm Scottish, lass. It is how we Scots all talk." He looked at her mother, winking. "Isn't that right, lass?"

Della's eyes widened. She had never heard of a Scot before, but before she could ask another question, a woman joined their small group, her cane tapping on the sidewalk. "Ron! Quit holding these people in the cold like this!"

"Mah apologies, Charlotte," Ron stated.

Della wasn't paying much attention to the words around her any longer but to the woman now, taking in her dark dress and hair that she had piled up on her head, her silver combs twinkling in the gaslight. Her gnarled hand clutched the cane and Della gasped at the glittering rings on each finger. The woman named Charlotte must have heard

Della's gasp for she peered at her. "Ye like my rings, gel?"

Della nodded quickly and the woman cackled with laughter. "Then ye have a fine eye indeed. My dear beloved Count Marchelle gave me these rings in exchange for my utter devotion. I can't bear to part with them."

Della didn't know who the Count was but the look on the older woman's face helped her understand that he must have been someone dear to her.

"I trust ye have a list?" Ron was asking her father, who swallowed hard.

"What sort of list?" he responded.

"Ye know, a list of those that are going tae make this easier for you," Ron explained. "This is debtor's prison, King's Bench, and ye have certain allowances as long as ye have supporters beyond these walls."

"Of, of course," her father said. "I can get a list straightaway."

"Come now," Charlotte was saying, waving her cane in the air before turning back to the building. "It is time to show you to your new lodgings."

Della's mother made a sound of distress, but her father was there in an instant, patting her hand. "It's going to be just fine, Iona, darling," he murmured. "We shan't be here long. I have friends, friends that will make this right."

Della didn't care who her father's friends were as long as they didn't make them stay here any longer than necessary. She wanted to go back to her own room, to Marcie, and forget that this had ever happened.

The family moved inside the doors and Della wrinkled her nose at the smell of refuse that hung heavily in the air. They moved up a set of rickety stairs, barely lit by the candles in the wall sconces, climbing higher until they reached a wooden landing. "This is your floor," Charlotte announced, her cane tapping along the hall. There was a low murmur of voices as they passed but it was too dark for Della to see where they were coming from. Shivering, she pressed herself tighter into her mother's skirts until finally Charlotte stopped before a door. "Ye might want tae reach out tae those supporters immediately," Ron said softly as Charlotte pushed open the door. "Tae send ye some comforts."

"Go on now," Charlotte was saying to Della's mother. Della watched as her mother straightened her shoulders and walked in, dragging Della with her. The room was no bigger than her own bedroom back at their home, with a narrow bed frame and a writing desk, the musty smell of the Thames drifting through the open window. "Mother?" Della asked, clutching her hand tightly. "What is this place?"

"Tis your new home," Charlotte replied, her hand on her hip as she eyed Della's mother. "And you aren't going to last a week."

"Enough, Charlotte," Ron said, his voice filling the void. "Don't frighten them so. They have had a terrible shock."

Charlotte huffed and whirled on her cane before marching out of the room.

"I will come tae gather that list for ye," Ron said finally as Della's father joined them. "Yer bags will be brought up directly."

Her father nodded and the door was shut, leaving the small family to their surroundings. "Oh Thomas!" her mother cried, releasing Della's hand to grip his. "We can't stay here! This is no place for us! No place at all!"

"I know, Iona," he said in a ragged breath. "But you have to give me time to fix this. I will ensure that we get everything we need in the meantime. We won't be here long. I promise you."

Della bit her lower lip as her mother cried in her father's arms. She had never seen her quite so upset before.

After her father comforted her mother and their bags arrived, he drew her into his arms. "I promise you, Della girl, that we won't be here long. You'll see. Everything will work out simply fine."

"I know," she sniffed as she laid her head on his shoulder. "You will fix everything, Papa." Her father wouldn't let her, and her mother, stay in a place like this. It wasn't their home. She wanted her mother to be happy again and her father to not look so worried.

But as she lay under a thin blanket on the bed later that evening, listening to her mother and father whisper in the dark, Della wasn't so certain that her father could fix this at all.

CHAPTER 2

*D*ella raced down the stairs, the chill of the morning penetrating her threadbare woollen coat as she did so. "Slow down child!" one of the women called out as she passed by, lugging a basket full of something back up the stairs.

Della didn't listen and in no time she was on the main landing of the prison, her boots colliding with the wooden floor. She loved mornings like this, where the prison was just beginning to awaken and before the noises started from the other side, where she wasn't allowed to be any longer. Della had been over there once, appalled at the iron bars instead of doors and the shrieks of those that were hidden in the shadows, filling her ears with sounds that had kept her from sleeping for a solid week.

Right now, the hall that connected the two buildings was quiet and she stole out of the side door into the courtyard between the two, breathing in the fresh air.

Well, as fresh as it could be, given she lived in a prison.

Through the fog that seemed to forever hang over the courtyard, Della could see the sun starting to rise over London, the many buildings that would soon awaken for the day. In a few short hours, the marketplace would be teeming with people and, despite her father's misgivings about her going there, Della had no plans to stay away.

The clatter of a hackney caught her attention and she hurried to the iron gates that surrounded the courtyard, gripping the cold metal between her hands. After five years of living at King's Bench, Della had made it her place to know everything she could regarding the comings and goings, including the new arrivals. While she had watched many come, there were very few that ever left the prison for good, unable to find a common place with those that they had owed funds to so that they could move on with their lives.

Della's own father was one of them. For years he had tried to get her and her mother out of this hovel, pleading to those that had once been business partners or friends of their family. Della had watched him scratch name after name off the list he kept on the desk, watching the parcels that had once come start to dwindle to nearly nothing.

If it weren't for Ron helping her father, Della knew that they wouldn't even have food, no matter how meagre it was now.

Heaving a breath, Della turned her attention back to the hackney, watching as a tall man in a long coat stepped out. When a small version of the man with straw coloured hair followed, Della smiled. Another child to join the small group that was here. She loved to play with the other children in the afternoons, even sharing in her chipped tea set with some of the younger girls so that they could pretend they were high born ladies in their drawing room on Mayfair Square. Her mother would often tell Della that she was foolish to think that way, but it didn't hurt to believe that one day perhaps they wouldn't be here any longer.

Not that Della missed her life before the prison. She could scarcely remember her bedroom or even the house that they had resided in. Her former nanny was merely a blurred memory to her and while she still had her porcelain doll and tea set, it was all that reminded her of that life before this.

Her mother, on the other hand, seemed to remember it more and Della had caught her more than once crying when she thought no one was looking.

Della's stomach rumbled which pulled her out of her thoughts, realising that the new arrivals had gone inside.

Drat. Pulling back from the iron bars, Della trudged across the empty courtyard and back to the door that would take her indoors. Perhaps later she would ask Charlotte who had arrived. Charlotte also knew everything regarding everyone and everything that happened in King's Bench and could tell Della whether or not the new arrival was worth Della's curiosity or not.

Della didn't have to wait long. The next day, when she was out walking the courtyard, she spied the boy from the morning prior doing the exact same, his hands shoved in his pockets. "Hey!" she called out, hurrying toward him. He glanced up at her, startled, and Della slowed her steps. Her mother was forever telling her to walk like a lady, but here, it didn't matter if you were a lady or not.

No one cared.

"Who are you?" she asked as he continued to watch her. "What is your crime?"

"My crime?" he echoed.

Della nodded. "I mean, not your crime, of course, but that of your family's. My father, he took a lot of money that he couldn't pay back and now we are here." She took in the fine wool of his coat, the way his brass buttons shined in the afternoon sun. "You are going to want to hide those. Brass brings in a good penny every now and again."

He looked down at his coat then back up to her. "My buttons? You are worried about my buttons?"

"Of course not," she scoffed, crossing her arms over her chest. "But you should be. Not everyone is as nice as I am." She had no need for his buttons, not wishing to take what belonged to another, no matter how desperate she became.

Others, they would not hesitate to rip those buttons off and probably more if it meant they could bargain outside the iron gates for a bit of food or a scrap of blanket.

"My father will not allow it," the boy said, straightening his thin shoulders. "I'm not afraid of anyone here."

Charlotte would say that he was one who wouldn't last a week, but Della held her tongue, not wanting to frighten him. He would find out soon enough that the prison was no place for talk like that. He was odd looking, sure enough, and a head taller than she was, with a nose that was far too big for his face and wide blue eyes that were fringed with the same colour that covered his head. "I'm Della," she said finally, extending her hand. "And I will be your friend."

He eyed her hand, the chipped nails that her mother was forever fretting over and the calluses on her palms, a testament to the hard labor she had done over the years. When his hand enveloped hers, Della smiled. "I'm Frederick," he said a moment later. "My father is the new turnkey."

The turnkey. Della's lips parted. "Your father is a prison guard?"

He nodded and Della's shoulders deflated. "Well, then, we won't be seeing much of each other," she said. The prisoners, herself included, were not allowed to mingle with the help.

Frederick continued to watch her with those large eyes of his. "But what if I want to see you?"

Della was tongue tied. "You want to see me?" she asked softly.

He shrugged, a dull flush spreading over his cheeks. "I didn't have many friends at the last prison, and I don't expect to have many here."

Della's heart went out to him, knowing how he felt. She had lost everything when her family had been forced to set foot in this prison and for the longest time, she had felt truly alone.

But as the years passed by, she realised that she could make something of this horrid life they had been given and that was what she had set out to do. "I would like that."

He grinned at her, and she returned his smile. Perhaps Frederick could help her pass the time as well.

A FEW MONTHS LATER, Della watched as her mother came down the stairs, coughing into her handkerchief as she did so. "I can do this, mother," she stated again, gripping the worn basket tightly in her hands. "I don't need you to accompany me."

"Of course, I will," her mother stated as she reached the landing, slightly out of breath. "Your father doesn't like it when you go to the marketplace alone."

Della knew that her father didn't like for them to go at all but over the past two months she had found that if she got in the right position at the marketplace, early in the mornings, she could sell all the flowers in her basket. The coins, however few she could gather, helped purchase a meat pie or two for her family, staving off the hunger pangs that came far too often now. Her father's list had no more names upon it, which meant that there were no more supporters for their cause.

They were going to perish in King's Bench and, even at her tender age, Della knew that hope was starting to fade.

If it weren't for Ron, who had just been freed a month prior, having paid off his debt, and Frederick, they would most certainly starve.

Della tried to ignore her mother's pale skin or the way she coughed nearly the entire time at the marketplace, helping her back to the prison with their small goods to share with her father. By the time they made it to their tiny room, sweat dotted her mother's forehead. "I just need to lie down," she murmured as Della pushed open the door. "I just need rest."

"Iona," her father stated, his eyes widening at the sight of his wife. "Dear God, what is wrong?"

"I just," her mother said before she collapsed against her husband. Della let out a cry, but her father waved her back, helping his wife to the bed. "Go get Charlotte," he said briskly.

Della raced out of the room and up the stairs to the fourth level, where Charlotte's room resided. She found the woman seated in the chair at her writing desk, her quill scratching over the paper. "Charlotte!" she cried out. "It is my mother."

Charlotte turned. "What is wrong with her?"

Della tried to catch her breath, but the tears clogged her throat and barely registered the older woman standing until she felt an arm around her shoulder. Somehow, even in King's Bench, Charlotte always smelt nice. "It is going to be all right," she said, pulling Della into her body. "We will see about your mother."

A few days later, Della leaned into the old woman once more as she watched her mother's body get draped with a sheet. "I'm sorry," Frederick said next to her, his hand clenched in hers. He had come once he had heard that Della's mother was sick, refusing to listen to Mr Marsh, the head overseer for King's Bench when he had ordered him away from the prisoners. Della was grateful that Frederick was here, having grown close to the gangly boy since his arrival. He didn't see her as a prisoner and while most of the others their age shied away from him, she hadn't.

"They are going to come get her soon," Charlotte murmured, her lips tightening. "They don't like for the dead to remain too long."

Though Della knew that Charlotte wasn't being cruel, the words were like a sharp blade to her already tortured heart. She glanced over at the chair in the corner, where her father sat, his eyes on her mother's still form. He hadn't said much since she had started taking her last breaths, refusing to eat or drink no matter how much Della pleaded.

Even Ron, who her father would listen to, couldn't get him to do anything but stare at the bed, his eyes red rimmed and face pale.

Her mother was gone, and it was only the two of them now. "We need to make certain she's presentable," Della said finally, moving from Charlotte's touch and Frederick's tight hold on her hand. Her mother's trunk was at the end of the bed and Della knew that her mother's silk gown, the same gown she had worn the night that they had come here, was carefully wrapped inside. It was the only thing that they hadn't parted with, her father refusing to allow her mother to sell it off, stating she should have some sort of reminder of what they would return to.

Now she would be buried in it.

As Della started to reach for the lid, Charlotte appeared at her side, pushing her hands away. "No," the older woman said softly. "You are far too young for this. I will take care of your mother, Della. Go on with Frederick."

Della held back a sob and Frederick was there to lead her out of the room, down the stairs and to the courtyard, where the sharp, crisp air filled her lungs. It wasn't fair that her mother had passed.

"Della, please," Frederick said, grasping her by the shoulders. "Tell me what you need."

Della turned in his arms and let out a sob as she threw her arms around his neck, nearly knocking him off his feet. "It's not fair!"

His arms circled around her, awkwardly brushing over her back. "I know. Go on, cry it all out."

So, Della did, but it wasn't nearly enough.

It never would be.

CHAPTER 3

*H*er mother's passing didn't end there. Della watched as her father grew listless, too stuck in his own grief to worry about their wellbeing. The letters didn't get written to their benefactors and her father quit conversing with anyone that happened by their little room.

Charlotte just clucked her tongue, a disapproving frown on her face. "He's going to let you starve to death, wallowing in his grief like that!" she remarked as she brought Della her rations of food for the day.

"He's missing my mother," she said softly to the old woman, her heart rending in her chest as she thought about never seeing her dearest mama again. She knew what that grief felt like. It was deep soul-searching grief, the kind that never truly went away no matter how many times she attempted to forget that her mother was truly gone.

Even at night, when the room was quiet and Della huddled under the desk on her blanket, her pillow a stuffed bag that had once held their belongings, she could hear her father sobbing in his sleep, calling out for the woman who had given up everything to wed him.

But as the weeks stretched into a month, Della too started to grow concerned that her father wasn't going to ever get over her mother's death.

"He's still huddled on the bed," she told Frederick one day as they returned from the market, the few coins from her flowers tucked safely in the pocket of her mended skirt. "I can't even get him to take a spoonful of soup."

"Do you want me to get my Pa to talk with him?" Frederick asked, pushing back the stray lock of hair that always seemed to fall on his forehead. Della sometimes wished to do it for him, to see if his hair was as soft and silky as it looked.

Frederick had become her constant companion, not caring that she was a prisoner and in such a condition that he should refrain from. He was much like his Pa, kind and always had a ready smile whenever she saw him. They had become best friends over the months since Frederick had arrived, and she was grateful that he was here now, helping her figure out what to do about her own father. "No," she said with a sigh. "It's not your problem to bear nor is it your Pa's. I'm just worried about Mr Marsh." And their future, but she didn't want to burden Frederick with that either.

Frederick kicked at a dirt clod with his boot, his hands shoved in his pockets. "You're not telling me something, Della."

He was right of course. She wasn't telling him that the meagre coins she made at market weren't enough to keep the food rations coming in. Mr Marsh had already happened by earlier in the day, wanting to know where their payment was for the room and warning her that he didn't give out charity in debtor's prison. If they couldn't continue to pay, then Della and her father would be escorted to the other side of King's Bench, the side that didn't have the already inadequate comforts she was used to right now.

The mere thought of being thrown into a cell with the rats caused Della to shudder involuntarily. "I don't know how to pay next month," she blurted out, causing Frederick to pause in his step. Tears welled in her eyes as he looked at her and she buried her face in her hands, letting them flow. "The money I have, is not enough."

"What about your father's benefactors?" Frederick asked softly as he drew her to his bony chest. "Have you written to them?"

Della shook her head, her face pressed up against his shirt now. Even despite the prison that he lived in, Frederick never failed to smell like sandalwood. "There's no one left to write to." Her father had wept over that bit of news a few days after her mother had passed on, getting a rejection from their last remaining benefactor.

"Oh, Della," Frederick murmured as he stroked her back lightly. "Why didn't you tell me?"

What could he do? He was only two years older than she, merely a boy still! Unless he knew a rich Londoner seeking a charitable case, it was hopeless.

Frederick pulled her back by her shoulders, his kind eyes searching hers. "I have an idea."

Della sniffled. "What sort of idea could you possibly have to help me, Frederick?"

He smiled. "I might not, but Charlotte will."

The two walked into the prison building and located the older woman on the second landing, her door was open as it tended to be during the daytime hours. Della had been down to Charlotte's quarters many times before, but whenever she did step through the door, she almost forgot that she was in a prison. The room itself was lavishly decorated, with curtains and a rug that Della didn't have in her own family's room. Charlotte herself was seated in an old velvet chair, her hands resting on her cane as she regarded them. "What is it?" she asked, tapping her cane once. "Can't you see that I am busy?"

Della looked about the room, noting that there was no one else around.

"Busy doing what?" Frederick asked, his voice full of false bravado. "Talking with ghosts?"

Charlotte cackled and Frederick took a step backward, nearly running into Della in the process. Della knew that Frederick was secretly afraid of the older woman, but he liked to put on a good face regardless. "Ghosts?" she echoed. "There aren't any ghosts here! Who would want to haunt a godforsaken place such as this?" Charlotte looked at her desk, which was littered with books and papers. "I'm working on my correspondence."

The two exchanged a look, knowing that Charlotte's response had always been just that. Della didn't know who continued to fund the older woman's place in King's Bench or why they didn't just pay her debts off and get her out of the prison. She had heard rumours about Charlotte, some even from Charlotte herself that she had been a consort to a powerful Viscount, who had caught her thieving and sent her to the prison, away from his home and his heart.

Given the looks of Charlotte's abode, someone was clearly taking care of her, and Della often wondered if it was still the viscount himself, having never forgotten his love.

"Della needs to earn funds," Frederick was saying, "or she will be forced to move to the other side of the prison."

Della shivered at the thought as Charlotte cackled. "So, your father is still being a spineless good for nothing?"

"He's grieving," Della shot back, her face burning with anger. "He's in no position to—"

Charlotte waved a bejewelled hand at Della. "Calm yourself, gel. I know what grieving is, but your father should come to realise that he has others to take care of."

Della didn't want to admit that she too was hurt by her father's lack of regard for her and their future. Without him, they were without any doubt going to be thrown into the prison proper.

Charlotte sighed loudly; her hands clasped on her cane. "What can you do, gel, besides run your mouth off?"

Della had long since learned not to take Charlotte's barbs to heart. "I can do all sorts of things," she started, her mind drawing a blank on what she could do. Her time in King's Bench had taught her a great many things, but there was much to learn.

"She's willing to find out," Frederick spoke up, nudging Della with his elbow. "I'm certain that she can get a position in one of the houses."

Charlotte eyed Della for a little longer before finally giving a single nod. "Go to Spring Gardens and make sure you steer clear of Mayfair."

"Why not Mayfair?" Della asked, curious.

"Because, gel," Charlotte snapped, her eyes flashing. "The dalliances will be fewer in Spring Gardens. The homes will have less servants, meaning no time for trysts and the like."

Della's cheeks coloured in embarrassment and Frederick cleared his throat. Charlotte could be quite blunt at times. While Della had not entertained that sort of idea, now she didn't want to have to encounter that at all.

"I will go," Frederick said after a moment, his eyes straying to Della's. "I will ask around for you."

"You will have to lie about her age," Charlotte pointed out. "No one will be willing to take on someone as young as you are. Tell them she's in her fourteenth year, boy, and don't open your trap about her being here. They will think she's a thief."

Della hated that her father's plight had such a bearing on her character. Why, she had never stolen anything before in her life, but because of where she was, everyone would assume she was a criminal.

When they finally left Charlotte, Frederick stopped Della on the stairs. "I will make certain to find you a good household," he stated, his chin lifted. "I will not put you in a place where you will find danger there."

Della gave Frederick a small smile, laying her hand on his arm. "I know you will, and I don't know what I can do to possibly repay you for all that you have done for me and my father."

Frederick covered her hand with his and Della was surprised by the jolt of warmth that she felt, hastily removing her hand from his arm. "I, well, I should check on father," she said in a rush, starting up the stairs.

"I will not let you down," Frederick called after her.

Della knew that he wouldn't, but for the rest of the day, she felt his touch on her hand and couldn't help but smile.

FREDERICK WAS true to his word. Three days passed before he found her in the prison courtyard, a buoyant smile on his face. "I did it!" he exclaimed. "I found you a position!"

Della listened with rapt attention as Frederick described the stately brick home in Spring Gardens, how the housekeeper was looking for a scullery maid that necessarily didn't need to remain at the home once their work was complete. Apparently, the home was already growing too small for all the staff that the lady of the house, The Dowager Countess of Benedict, Lady Benedict, required. "It's perfect, Della," Frederick replied. "You will see."

"I don't know what to say," Della responded slowly as Frederick grinned at her. "Whatever would I do without you?"

"Well," he started, drawing out the word. "You would be a bit bored here, all by yourself."

She elbowed him in the stomach, a smile on her face. "Perhaps, or perhaps I will be better off without the likes of you pestering me so."

Her tone was light as she said the words, profoundly grateful for his friendship. King's Bench was a lonely place to be at times and despite their differences, Frederick didn't see her as a prisoner but as a friend. "When do I start?"

"Tomorrow morning," he replied, hooking his thumbs into the loops on his pants. "Promptly at five."

Della's smile faded. There was no way that Mr Marsh was going to open the gate for her at that time of the morning. "Frederick, I…"

He waved a hand at her. "I already know what you are going to say and once I speak to father, he will allow it, I swear to you."

Della had her doubts, but the next morning she dressed in the cold as quietly as she could, hurrying down the stairs to the front door. Frederick was lounging against the doorway as she approached, handing her a wrapped bundle. "Here," he said softly, his voice still groggy from sleep. "It is bread and cheese for you to break your fast with."

Her eyes filled with tears, and she threw her arms around him, feeling him clasp her tightly against his upper body. "Frederick, thank you for everything."

He cleared his throat as she pulled back and, even in the pre-dawn light, Della could see the faint blush across his bony cheeks. "Go on with you now. I expect a full report this evening."

Della gave him one last smile as she slipped through the door, finding the gate already unlocked that would lead to the dirty sidewalk. This was going to turn her, and her father's, fortunes around, perhaps even help them continue to pay back the funds he had lost to his debtors.

A FEW DAYS LATER, Della was all but ready to give up. The work as a scullery maid was far more difficult than selling flowers at the market, and despite her best efforts, she never seemed to do anything right. The other maids seemed to resent the fact that she had come to the household and Della barely held her tears at bay when she left in the evening, making the long trek back to the prison before Mr Marsh locked her out.

Frederick was always there in the mornings with a kind word and a bit of breakfast and each evening he listened to her talk about what had happened that day, telling her not to give up.

This evening was no different. Della walked up the stairs to the front door, feeling her body ache from the constant stooping and carrying of heavy items up and down the steep stairs. Frederick was there, holding something in his hands.

When he saw her tearstained cheeks, his expression fell. "No better?"

She shook her head, a fresh set of tears threatening. "I don't know if I can continue to do this, Frederick! Perhaps I'm meant for the other side."

"Of course not," he scolded, drawing her into the courtyard instead of inside the building. "I have something for you, Della."

Della watched as Frederick unfurled his hand and a baby mouse lay there, his whiskers twitching at the sudden rush of cool air. "Oh my!" she breathed, clasping her hands to her chest, and promptly forgetting about her worries. "It's so sweet!"

"I'm calling it, Tiny," Frederick said proudly, stroking the tiny head with the tip of his finger. "If this little guy can survive in such a harsh world, so can you, Della."

Della watched as Frederick coddled the mouse, realising that he was right. She had come too far to just give up and prove to everyone that she wasn't as strong as they thought.

She wouldn't give up, if nothing else but for her only friend that had so much faith in her ability.

CHAPTER 4

FIVE YEARS LATER...

*D*ella blew the stray hairs out of her face as she stirred the white shirts in the pot of boiling water, feeling the sweat slip down the back of her woollen dress. Laundry day was simply the worst and Della had learned to detest the chore. Her hands stung from the strong lye soap she had used to wash the shirts and reddened from the hot water. If it hadn't been for Charlotte's soothing balm that she had given Della, her hands would be far worse.

"Are you done yet?"

Della looked up to find one of the other maids, Juliette, standing in the doorway, her mop cap askew. It always was, no matter how many times the girl straightened it. "Almost," she stated, putting aside the paddle. "Come, help me get them out."

Together, the two women were able to pull them out of the water and hang them on the drying rack near the fire, not too close in case there was a spark. After banking some of the fire, Della wiped her hands on her apron. "Now, I'm done."

"Good," Juliette remarked. "Because I am starving and cook says there are scones left from the morning, if we hurry."

Della giggled and they hurried up the stairs to the main level of the townhouse, crossing the hall before anyone could see them to head down to the kitchens. Sure enough, cook was setting a platter of scones out the moment they arrived, and Della smiled as she saw the empty table. The others hadn't made it to luncheon yet, meaning that she and Juliette could have their pick of the scones. "Careful now," cook said as she reached for the pot on the stove. "They've just come out the oven so they might be a bit hot."

"I don't care," Juliette announced, grabbing one before taking a bite of it.

Della was a bit more careful with hers, setting it on the tin plate that she would have her luncheon on. Perhaps she would only eat half of it and take the other to her father, giving him a reason to smile today. He enjoyed it when she brought morsels of food back from her employer, reminiscent of their former life. Della had been fortunate herself to hold her position at the widow, Lady Benedict's home for the past five years, learning all that she could about how to properly manage a household. Whereas she had started out as a scullery maid, now she was learning how to be a housekeeper, hoping that one day she would take over.

It wasn't that bad working for Lady Benedict. Della had learned long ago that the woman was like many other upper-class Londoners, crass and snobbish, but overall good to her household staff. The others that came and went told stories about the other households they had served in, and Della was glad that she had started here.

"I swear! One moment she wants her pearls, the next diamonds. It's not like the king is going to knock on her door."

Della hid her smile as two of the widow's lady's maids came into the kitchen, their uniforms crisp and starched, just as their employer required. Della's own uniform had wilted from her time spent with the laundry and she knew she would have to work on the wrinkles before the next day.

Suzette plopped in the seat next to Della and snatched the largest scone from the platter. "Well, she is still young compared to other widows. You would think all those parties she attends would help her find a husband."

Pauline joined them, wrinkling her nose at the scones. Della knew that the young woman detested the pastries. "Well, when one has nothing but sons, she's in no hurry to support a season I guess."

"It's not true," Juliette replied, frowning. "You are forgetting her daughter."

The two ladies' maids laughed. "Truly?" Suzette asked, her eyes twinkling in laughter. "Lady Christine is over her thirtieth year, at least. The only husband she is going to find is the one with one foot in the grave and with those looks, she will have to find a blind one!"

They laughed again and Della managed a smile. It wasn't nice at all to talk about others in such a manner, but Lady Christine was an odd duck, if one could be labeled as such. She kept to her rooms on the third floor of the residence and in the five years that Della had worked here, she had only seen the woman twice.

"Either way," Pauline stated, her eyes gleaming. "It would be good for Lady Benedict to step out in style this social season. Perhaps she can find someone to warm her bed and carve some of the ice off her."

Della tried not to sigh at the thought. If her father hadn't committed the crimes years ago, she would be preparing for her own first London season. Though they weren't the upper crust of society, her father had at least made it seem that they had enough funds that would support a small season at least.

Now, she barely had enough funds to pay Mr Marsh each month, especially since the price continued to go up every year. He had explained it as interest on the money that her father owed, but Della wasn't so certain. She knew that he wasn't overly fond of her friendship with Frederick and the liberties that he was able to give her to keep this position.

"Well," Juliette stated, polishing off the last bite of her scone as the cook started to dole out the hearty stew made from last night's dinner leftovers. "I for one, would have no qualms about catching a Viscount, at the very least."

Suzette snickered. "How? By telling him of your pure virtue? We all know how much of your time is spent in the carriage house with William."

Della joined the others in a quick laugh as Juliette threw her napkin at the lady's maid. "It could happen."

"No one sees us," Suzette said softly, her brow furrowed. "We're nothing but hired help. No gentleman is going to turn his head in our direction."

"My mother did," Della said softly, causing the entire table to look in her direction. "My father was a footman, and my mother was part of the upper-crust of Scottish society."

"Really?" Juliette asked, her eyes rounding. "You've never told me that."

She hadn't told anyone truly. Frederick knew of course and Charlotte too, but they were what she considered her family.

"There's nothing much to say."

"Why of course there is!" Pauline spoke up. "You shouldn't be here then. You should be hobnobbing with the richies."

Della laughed and shook her head. "Oh no, I'm far from the ballroom."

"Why is that?" Cook asked as she joined the rest of them at the table and picking up her spoon. "Sounds to me as if you're royalty yerself, so why are you here?"

Della swallowed, wishing she had never said anything to begin with. No one in the household knew her story, where she stayed, nothing. She had kept that to herself. "We fell on bad times," she chose instead.

"Who cares?" Juliette replied, throwing up her hands. "I want to hear how your father roped in your mother instead."

So, Della told her favourite story, how her mother had come home from finishing school to find her father having been hired on by Della's grandfather. She told the captive audience how her mother had sworn it was love at first sight but given her station, she had to ignore what was in her heart for nearly a year until her father had confessed his own feelings to her one night under the stars.

She hadn't told her parents and they carried on an illicit liaison for months until finally her father had gathered enough coin to get them to Gretna Green. "She married him with barely a farthing to his name," she finished, her chest aching at the thought of her mother and how she had died far too soon. "And never looked back."

The group was silent for a few moments before the cook hit her spoon on the table. "Get yer heads out of the clouds and eat up! There's nary a noble gent coming down here to make yer acquaintance!"

Della picked up her spoon, her parents' story still fresh on her mind. Her mother had loved her father, but in the end, it had been her demise. Where would her mother be if she hadn't run away with her father? Likely in a castle in Scotland, as she was destined to be the lady of.

One thing was for certain, Della wouldn't be seated at this table had her mother decided to take another direction in her life and likely neither would her father be in debtor's prison.

"Well, I hear that Lord Benedict is due to arrive any day now," Pauline stated once they had finished their meal. "He's positively handsome."

"Yer mooning eyes aren't going to draw him in," Juliette muttered as she carried her bowl to the sink for washing. "He's looking for a titled woman. His mother won't allow anything less."

Pauline batted her eyes at the lot of them. "Never hurts to try, right?"

Della finished her meal quickly and placed her plate in the sink as well. She didn't care to talk about gentlemen or the latest gossip amongst the servants. She only wished to complete her tasks and go back to her father.

That afternoon, she was assigned to dusting the lower floor of the house, taking her feather duster and running it over the priceless objects in the drawing room. Lady Benedict enjoyed her collections, and she had quite the assortment of figurines of all shapes and sizes.

Still, it was nice to be away from the others. While she enjoyed the other servants the household, Della truly didn't fit in with them. Many had been raised in the East End of London, barely scraping by to feed their families and provide a roof over their heads. Now Della could relate somewhat by being in debtor's prison, but she knew that she couldn't walk into East End and be accepted. Her manners were far too refined… and her dreams, she didn't want to think about her dreams.

For they were nothing more than that. Dreams that wouldn't come to light now, dreams of one day walking away from King's Bench with her arm linked with her father's and even going back to the wilds of Scotland to meet her mother's family.

She would wear modest gowns and find a gentleman that would love her for her intellect and not the titles she would never hold.

That was what she wished to have, though they were all farfetched. It was likely she would be at King's Bench until she died.

"Della."

Della turned to find the housekeeper at the door, her hands twisting in her apron nervously. "Yes, ma'am?"

"Lady Benedict wants to see you upstairs," she answered. "What did you do, gel?"

"N...nothing," Della stammered as she placed her feather duster in her pocket. "I swear it."

The housekeeper sighed. "Go on with you then. She's waiting."

Della curtseyed and hurried up the stairs, the polished wooden bannister slick under her hand. She didn't venture up the stairs often, but Della knew where the widow's suite of rooms were from memorising the layout of the home during one of her first days there. On the opposite end of the hall was where her son slept whenever he came home and many a maid had blushed when they had been assigned to tend to his rooms.

Della would rather do laundry any day of the week.

She knocked on the closed door politely and it opened to reveal Pauline. "She wants to hear about your mother," Pauline said softly as she admitted Della into the lavish suite. "Suzette told her the story."

Della's stomach twisted at the thought of what Lady Benedict could want. This was why she shouldn't have said anything to anyone save Frederick and Charlotte, who knew all there was to know about Della and her plight.

Lady Benedict sat on her chaise lounge; her sprigged muslin skirts spread about her. She was still a stately woman given her age, with her grey streaked dark hair and the glittering jewels around her neck and on her fingers. Now, Della understood what they were discussing at luncheon.

"This is Della, milady," Suzette replied, giving Della a nod. "She's the one who told us the story."

"Della," Lady Benedict replied as Della curtseyed. "I hear that your mother was of good pedigree."

"Yes, my lady," Della responded, clutching the fringes of her apron tightly in her grasp. "She was a Scottish lady."

"Ah," the widow said, tapping her finger against her cheek. "And your father was a footman you say?"

Cheeks flushed, Della could only nod. Her father was much more than that now, even with his transgressions that had laid them in King's Bench. He just missed her mother so much that it was hard for him to do anything. Della could carry the burden for them.

"Well, then," her employer finally stated, gesturing toward a floral printed chair next to her. "Please take a seat. I would like to hear the story myself."

Della couldn't possibly refuse the woman who provided for her and her father, so she did as she was asked, clutching her hands in her lap. Lady Benedict called for tea and Suzette rushed to do her bidding as Della started to tell her parents' tale, as they had told it to her when she was younger. "Positively scandalous!" the widow exclaimed as Della ended the story with them in London and her mother dying, though she didn't say where. The last thing she needed was for them to learn where she lived. "And now look at you, here in my employ. Tell me, Della, do you enjoy your work?"

"Yes, my lady," she said quickly, ducking her head as Suzette arrived with the delicate tea set and some of the scones from earlier. "You have been very kind to me."

Lady Benedict smiled. "Well, I would like for you to repay that kindness by entertaining a few friends of mine with your story an hour from now. Can you do that for me?"

Della saw the gleam in the woman's eye and wished she could decline. The only reason that the widow wished to hear the tale again would be to poke fun at her and her family origins. "Yes, my lady," she said softly, keeping the anger out of her voice.

"Good!" the widow exclaimed, clapping her hands. "Suzette, serve Della some tea so she might refresh herself before they arrive, and be quick about it!"

Suzette did as she was asked, her apologetic eyes meeting Della's. Della took the delicate cup and saucer without acknowledging it. She was upset that Suzette thought it was fine to tell her own personal business but more so upset with herself that she had divulged it to a group of gossiping women.

Now she would be forced to endure a dreadful afternoon.

CHAPTER 5

The shadows were lengthening through the windows by the time the widow's acquaintances left the formal parlour. Della's shoulders slumped, her voice raw from the re-telling and her ears burning from the tittering of laughter and ribald comments that were made about her mother. Never in her life had she been so embarrassed.

"Well," Lady Benedict said finally, clasping her hands in her skirts. "You did well, Della. Exactly what I asked you to do. I hear that you have a chance to become housekeeper one day. Is that correct?"

"Yes, my lady," Della replied, drawing in a breath as the widow eyed her. She wanted nothing more than to leave this household and go back to King's Bench, where she knew there would be no judgement, only sympathy. Frederick would be waiting for her by the gate with a kind word and she would tell him about her day before visiting with her father before their meagre dinner.

"Then perhaps you will succeed quicker than you planned," her employer finished. "You may go now, Della."

Della rose to leave the room, but her exit was suddenly blocked by a tall gentleman in a fine blue coat and piercing hazel eyes. "Who might you be?" he asked lightly, his eyes alight with laughter.

"Theo!" the widow cried, rising from her perch. "I wasn't expecting you until tomorrow!"

So, this was Lord Benedict. He was quite handsome, with light brown hair that hung over his broad forehead and a strong jawline that many a woman would swoon over. His clothing was of fine material, right down to his boots. Della swallowed as he took a step forward into the room. "Mother, who is this?"

"Oh," his mother stated, waving a bejewelled hand at him. "This is Della, one of our house maids. She was just entertaining me with a story of her family. Do you know that her mother was a Scottish society lady?"

"Oh?" Lord Benedict replied, arching a brow. "I believe I would like to hear the story too."

Della swallowed. She didn't want to relive the story for the third time today.

"Of course," Lady Benedict stated. "Come sit, Della, and give my son your account."

"I will be grateful for your words," Lord Benedict added, catching Della by surprise. He looked so earnest that she had no choice but to turn on her heel and walk back to the chair as the young gentleman settled himself next to his mother. She watched as the widow lit up and pressed her lips to her son's hand. Lady Benedict looked clearly happy to see her son and Della's heart softened a little. She could entertain them for few moments longer.

She launched into her story but only got a few minutes into it before he held up his hand. "I can tell that you are from Scottish descent," he said, his smile warm. "You have the fire in your eyes."

Della blushed under his praise. "My mother always said that I had fire in my veins, my lord."

"I believe it," Lord Benedict replied with a smile. "Go on."

Flustered now, Della found her place and continued, not at all surprised when Lord Benedict held up his hand once more to halt her words. "Tell me more about your father," he urged.

"Theodore!" his mother replied, clearly not at all happy that he kept interrupting Della. "Let the young woman tell her story and be done with it! We don't have all day."

"I want to hear about her father," Lord Benedict said calmly, giving his mother a placating smile. "It is the favourite part of her story after all. Don't you see how her eyes light up when she talks about him?"

It was true. While Della loved her mother, her father was now her everything. She was the one who was taking care of him, the one who had taken it upon herself to ensure that his debts continued to be paid. Without him, Della didn't know what she would do.

So, she told the stories she knew about her father, how he had worked hard to become a husband that he thought her mother deserved. Lord Benedict's eyes never left hers, even when she teared up for a moment, stopping to compose herself.

When the last word left her lips, Lady Benedict clapped her hands, displeasure written all over her face that Della had kept them for so long. "That's enough, Della. You've entertained me enough on this day. Go and see about your duties before you are dismissed for the day."

"Yes, my lady," Della stated, glad to escape the parlour at last. The housekeeper was the first to see her in the hallway. "What did she want?" she hissed as Della hurried past. "You were with her all afternoon."

"She wished to hear the nature of my family," Della replied, keeping her tears at bay. She was exhausted from retelling her family's plight and only wished to leave this place as soon as she could.

"Your family?" the housekeeper questioned but her words fell on deaf ears as Della moved on, keeping to herself as she completed the rest of her duties before she was allowed to leave for the evening.

As she was leaving by the servant's entrance, a hand fell on her arm and Della looked up, shocked to find the spinster sister staring down at her with her oddly coloured green eyes. "He's enthralled with you," Lady Christine said quickly, her eyes darting about. "If you are smart, you will run."

"Whatever are you talking about?" Della stated, wincing as the woman's grip grew tighter. "Who?"

"Careful, girl," Lady Christine said instead, finally removing her hand from Della's arm. Della was certain there would be an imprint on her skin once she removed her dress. "Careful."

Before Della could ask any more questions, the lady turned and darted up the stairs quickly, leaving Della to stare after her. It was the oddest interaction she'd ever had.

Dusk was fast approaching by the time Della made it to King's Bench and, despite the fact she was nothing more than a prisoner there, she loosened a breath. It wasn't much of a home, but here there were no nosy nobles trying to make fun of her.

Frederick was standing by the gate as Della made her way down the sidewalk, his hands in his trouser pockets. The years had been kind to Frederick, helping him fill out his gangly form and sharp contours of his face, though he kept his strong jawline covered in what she affectionately referred to as his attempt to grow facial hair. His shoulders were now broad, filling the coarse linen shirts he preferred, and she knew that there were more muscles underneath his clothing from his days helping his father around the prison. Everyone loved Frederick and Della wondered why he was still here. She knew that his father had offered to send him anywhere he liked, even procuring a letter from a noble if he chose to go to Eton, but Frederick declined them all. While Della was grateful that her closest friend was still here, she knew it was only a matter of time before he moved on. He had no interest in following in his father's footsteps and soon a young woman would catch his eye, pulling him from the prison and away from her.

It is only fitting, she thought, as she reached the gate, that he too would leave.

"You're late," Frederick said softly as he pushed away from the gate. "I had to convince Mr Marsh to leave it open and not send the authorities after you."

"I had a trying day," Della said as they walked through so that Frederick could latch it shut. She watched with cool detachment as he ran the length of the chain around the bars and pushed the padlock closed, where it would remain until the morning. "I will apologise to Mr Marsh."

Frederick ran a hand through his hair roughly and Della resisted the urge to smooth it down for him. "Dell, are you all right? I mean did something happen at that widow's residence?"

Della thought back to the day, where Lord Benedict showed up and ruined what was a peaceful existence for her. Well, that and the fact that she had thought it smart to share her family's personal strife. Now she was the talk of the household and knew that one day was not going to make it all disappear. "It's fine," she bit out, not wanting him to worry. "Nothing I can't handle."

"I've been thinking," Frederick continued as they climbed the stone steps to the building. "Of my future."

"It's about time," she muttered, pausing just inside. "You are going to take your father's suggestion of going to Eton, aren't you?"

Frederick's eyes widened. "What? No, I don't belong with those rich idiots. I have no interest in becoming a toff. I've been thinking about a different sort of future, Dell."

Della sighed. "Your words are increasing my already aching head, Frederick. Can we discuss this later?" All she wished to do was go upstairs and sleep for the few remaining hours she had before it was time to go back to the residence again.

Frederick took a step toward her. "Dell, this is important. I've held off long enough."

"Frederick, please," Della replied softly, reaching out to touch his arm. "I need to check on father and ensure he's eaten his supper. Dawn will come far too quickly."

His jaw tightened but he finally stepped back. "All right. Another time, perhaps."

She gave him a tired smile. "Thank you. Good night."

"Good night, Della."

When Della entered their small room, her father was already abed, and she didn't bother to wake him. If she did, Della knew she would see her father's red rimmed eyes and haunted look about him, the same one he wore seemingly every day. She couldn't remember the last time she had heard him laugh, seen him smile, anything other than the despair he had fallen into and stayed in.

With a sigh, she ate her paltry ration of food, some stale bread and an apple that was only slightly bruised on one side, before undressing and lying down on the small mattress that Frederick had procured for her a few years ago. The blanket did nothing to help provide warmth for her chilled bones and the coal fireplace had burned out hours ago, but Della knew how to ignore those plights.

Instead, she thought about Lord Benedict and how his gaze hadn't strayed far from her face earlier, how he seemed to truly be interested in her story and would have held her there longer had the widow not shooed her off.

Snorting, Della tucked her hands under her cheek. Lord Benedict was a noble, a gentleman with better things to do than to even think about her after she had walked out of the room. There were rumours that he would be looking for a wife once he returned to London and, with the social season fast approaching, Della assumed that was why he had come back from his travels.

Well, she would be certain to make herself scarce for the next few days to both Lord Benedict and the widow.

And Lady Christine. The exchange with the spinster this evening had been completely out of the blue and a little disturbing. What had the woman been talking about? What had she seen that had made her seek out Della?

Likely nothing. Just another way to get Della riled up by yet another member of the family. Della wished she could wash her hands of them all.

She couldn't of course. The money she was paid was keeping the hunger at bay and the creditors at least tolerable.

And Frederick. Della thought of her friend, how he had insisted she listen to him before finally letting her leave. Something was bothering him, and it would have been the right thing to do to listen to him. Frederick had made her life here tolerable over the years, keeping Mr Marsh at bay and providing comforts when Della had no means to pay. If it weren't for Frederick and Charlotte both, Della would have never made it this far.

She would apologise to him in the morning, Della decided as her eyes started to grow heavy with sleep. The last thing she needed was for him to be upset with her. He was her true friend, the only one in this wretched place she could count on.

That night, however, Della's dreams were filled with the probing gaze of Lord Benedict...

CHAPTER 6

The next morning came far too quickly and Della was barely awake herself when she walked to the gate, seeing Frederick was waiting there as he always was, a steaming hunk of bread slathered in jam for her. "I'm sorry," she said in a rush as he handed the bread over to her. "About yesterday."

"It's all right." Frederick sighed, giving her a small smile. "But you will allow me to explain myself this evening, perhaps?"

She gave him a tired smile. "Perhaps."

Della bit into the bread and moaned as the explosion of the tart fruit danced over her tongue. "This is heavenly," she exclaimed, finishing it up quickly before dusting the crumbs off her gloves. "You are far too good to me Frederick."

Frederick didn't respond as he removed the lock and chain, opening the gate. "I will wait for you this evening."

Della gave him a little wave and hurried to the Benedict residence, letting herself in through the servant's entrance. It was her turn to light the fires in the rooms on the main floor, as well as the kitchen so that the cook could start the morning meal. Hurriedly she stripped off her layers of clothing to ward against the cold and made certain to do the kitchen first, carrying the flint to the receiving room next. The footman had already laid out the wood in the fireplace for her, a request of the widow instead of the long burning coal, and Della knelt, using a piece of old newspaper to help the flame catch.

As the fire flared to life, Della allowed herself a brief moment to warm her own cold fingers. What luxury it was to wake every morning with a warm room to greet you! The coals were burned down to nothing when she had woken this morning, her breath easily seen in the cold room as she had got dressed and used the last bit to coax the fire in the grate to life for her father.

Then she had thrown her own blanket over his quaking shoulders, hoping that the additional layer would stave off the cold for a little longer. While he would have the comfort of the warm room, Della knew that by the time she hurried home, it would be cold again.

With a sigh, Della forced herself to move. There were six other fireplaces to be lit, not including the ones on the second level that the ladies' maids would handle. Then it would be up to the footmen to ensure that they remained lit throughout the day.

Della hurried to the study. Though it wasn't a room she normally tended to, since Lord Benedict was back, he would likely wish to use the room now and she wasn't going to be the one that was chastised for not having it prepared for him.

As she opened the door, she was startled to find the blaze already going and a silhouette standing before it, a drink in his hand. "Della," he said, a look of surprise on his handsome face. "Whatever are you doing here?"

"Lighting the fires, my lord," she forced out, showing him the flint. "But I see that this one is already lit."

He smiled and Della attempted to ignore the fluttering of her stomach at the sight. He had clearly not been to bed yet, his cravat loose and hanging about his neck, the top buttons on his fine shirt unbuttoned to show the tanned skin underneath. His evening coat was draped over one of the wing-backed chairs near the fire and she wondered if he had just stepped foot inside the residence before she had. "I confess," he was saying, placing the glass on the mantle, "in my travels, I've lit many a fire myself."

"I should go finish the rest," she stammered, backing toward the door. "My apologies for bothering you, my lord." It wasn't proper to be in the same room together if she valued her virtue. She had heard stories from the passing employees that came in and out of the residence over the years, stories of how the master, and sometimes the mistress, of the home would seek their pleasure in those that had nowhere else to go. Some were prepared with ways to prevent falling with child, but others, well, they found a babe in their belly and turned out on their ear.

She didn't wish to find herself in that sort of predicament.

"No, wait," Lord Benedict stated as Della turned to go. "Please, stay. I only wish to talk to you. You are safe with me, Della."

"You should be abed," she replied, clapping her hand over her mouth as she realised what she had just said. "I… I apologise."

He waved a hand at her. "No, thank you for being so observant. You are right, of course. I should be abed." His grin caused Della's body to warm all over and her cheeks flushed. "I confess it's difficult when I come back to London to not partake in the revelry around me."

Della imagined that he had spent much of his evening in the clubs and gambling dens that gentlemen tended to frequent. "Then I will leave you to your drink, my lord," she said quickly, turning and fleeing from the room before he could stop her once more. Now Della knew that since Lord Benedict had taken a shine to her for some odd reason, she would need to be far more aware than ever to not put herself in a compromising position.

If she lost her position, she and her father would be escorted out of their small room and to a prison cell, until they starved to death.

Lucky for Della, she was able to complete her duties without any interference from anyone else in the residence, even deciding to take her luncheon outside to avoid the whispers and stares from the other servants. She detested the fact that she had been singled out by the widow and Lord Benedict, which made everyone even more curious about her, whereas all she wished to do was earn her wages and take care of her father.

When she arrived back at King's Bench, it wasn't Frederick who was waiting for her but Ron. "Ron!" she called out, a smile on her face. The big scot gave her a friendly wave as she walked into the gate before wrapping her into one of his famous embraces. "Della, lass, ye have grown so."

"You shouldn't have stayed away for three years," she teased him. "Have you come to see father?"

He nodded. "I was in town on some business and thought ye could use a visitor."

Her smile faded. "He's not doing well, Ron."

Ron clucked his tongue as he linked arms with her. "Well, now, let's see wot I can do."

Della allowed him to escort her inside, seeing Frederick coming toward them. "Ron," Frederick acknowledged, his gaze flickering over Della.

"Wee Frederick," Ron replied with a grin. "We were on our way tae see Thomas. Would ye like tae join us?"

Della watched as Frederick swallowed before shaking his head. "I'm off to do an errand for my father. Enjoy your visit."

Her lips parted, remembering that Frederick wished to speak to her, but he had gone through the door before she could call after him.

"Wot's wrong with him?" Ron asked, a frown marring his face.

Della shrugged. "I'm not certain. Come, let's go upstairs."

Her father was seated on the side of the bed when they walked in, his eyes lighting as he saw his friend. "Ron Fraser, do my eyes deceive me?"

"Nay," Ron chuckled as her father struggled to stand. Della detested seeing her father's clothing hanging off his body in such a manner, knowing that he wasn't eating nearly enough to keep up his strength.

He looked nothing like the man from her childhood, and more like the starving prisoners from the other side of King's Bench.

"Come, sit," she said hurriedly, pulling the chair out from under the desk. On the scarred top were the letters her father had started to any possible benefactors, and her eyes teared as she read his desperate words. He was trying, but she knew that some days were better than others.

Ron sat in the rickety chair and her father leaned forward eagerly. "Tell me all your news," he stated, looking a bit more interested than he had been in quite some time.

It warmed her heart.

So, Della left the room to allow the two men to discuss the latest news from London and walked down the flight of stairs to Charlotte's room. She found the older woman seated in her chair, reading the latest salacious romance novel that she had somehow got her hands on. "What is on your mind, child?" she asked immediately as soon as Della walked in. "That lout of a father finally decide to take up his responsibilities?"

Della shook her head. Charlotte had told her often enough that her father was lazy and inadequate to allow Della to be the one to support them both and no matter how many times she had tried to defend her father, the woman wasn't hearing it. "Ron is visiting."

Charlotte's pale eyes lifted, and a smile spread over her face. "I did love that Scot. He reminded me of my first paramour. That man, he could make me blush like a young maiden when he removed his clothes."

Della did the blushing for the older woman. By now she should be used to the way that Charlotte spoke so candidly about her life before King's Bench, but it never ceased to amaze her how she could surprise her when she thought she had heard it all.

"Sit," Charlotte demanded, pointing to her bed. "Something is bothering you or you wouldn't be visiting me."

Della did as Charlotte demanded, clasping her hands tightly in her lap. "Did you ever find yourself the subject of gossip?"

Charlotte cackled with laughter. "Of course, I did! I was a paramour, a mistress, my darling girl. I was forever in the social rags and whispered about in the ballrooms of the famed London season."

Della swallowed hard. "How did you move past it?" She had aptly avoided the household, but she couldn't do it forever, not if she wished to keep her position.

The older woman eyed her. "What sort of trouble have you got yourself into? Did you let someone take liberties with you?"

Della blushed. "N... no of course not. I told the others of my family's plight and it's caught the attention of Lady Benedict and her son." It pained her to think about her interaction with Lord Benedict this very morning and how it seemed he wanted more from her.

"Ah," Charlotte concluded, understanding dawning on her wrinkled face. "It will flutter in the wind like most gossip does. You just have to walk in with your head held high and show them that you cannot be bothered with idle gossip." She narrowed her gaze. "This son, he's caught your attention."

"More like the other way around," Della muttered.

"Have I ever told you the story of how I became a mistress?" Charlotte stated after a moment. Instead of waiting for Della's reply, she continued. "I was naive, thinking that I could garner the riches of London society by giving away the most important bargaining chip that a woman has. The gentleman was a smooth talker, promising me a title and a place by his side if only I would warm his bed." Her expression grew wistful. "I did exactly what he wished and paid the ultimate price."

"I'm not going to allow that to happen to me," Della said softly.

"Perhaps not, "Charlotte declared. "But sometimes you can't help but fall victim to the trappings of your tender heart. Do you think I wished to become a whore, girl?" Charlotte sighed. "I wanted love, a family, a title. What I got was a title that no one would associate with and riches that couldn't buy me the family I wanted."

Della left Charlotte shortly afterward, moving into the prison courtyard instead of heading back to the room just yet. She was hoping that Ron's visit would spur something in her father to bring him back to the living. She needed her father.

What she didn't need was any more attention from Lord Benedict or his mother. She did not belong in their world, or their attention, other than as their servant.

When she arrived at the household the next morning to light the fires, Della was relieved not to find Lord Benedict in the study again. It wasn't until she decided to partake in her luncheon in the kitchen that she found out why.

"I hear he's been sent to the country estate," Juliette replied as she nibbled on her bread, left over from the morning calls. "The widow was none too pleased to hear of his exploits to date."

Something in Della's shoulders eased as she picked at her own sandwich.

"But he's just got here!" Pauline stated, visibly upset that she would not have her time with the handsome lord. "How I am ever to batt my lashes to a man who isn't even there!"

"Like you had a chance to begin with," Cook grumbled, seating herself in the empty chair. "Eat you flock of pigeons."

Della did as she instructed. At least she didn't have to worry about running into him any time soon.

CHAPTER 7

*T*he next few weeks were uneventful.

Della rose each morning to make her trek to the residence and each evening returning to the prison with a few coins in her pocket to turn into the man who collected their debts. Her father was still as morose as he had been, seemingly more so since Ron's visit and Della tried not to push him. She couldn't understand his grief, as it had been years since her mother had passed on and she herself, had moved on.

She needed him to do the same.

Still, he was able to write a few letters looking for support to a few potential benefactors, but none were answered, much to his dismay.

It seemed that they had been forgotten about.

Della knew it was no longer an option to allow others to care for them. Her father was no longer the clerk that was favoured by so many, nothing more than a guilty party now that he couldn't get himself out of debtor's prison, even after all this time.

Why would anyone wish to help them? They were nothing more than commoners now, a name that would cease to exist when they perished in prison.

Frederick still met Della each morning with a small breakfast, but something was different about her friend, something that he refused to discuss. Gone were his kind smiles and witty banter, almost as if Della was now just another chore that he had to attend to and while she wanted to ask Frederick what the issue was, he never gave her a moment to do so.

One evening, as Della trudged back to the prison, she found Mr Marsh waiting for her at the gate instead of Frederick. "Della," he said, his beady eyes on her form as she entered. "You are on time this evening."

"Yes, sir," she replied, clutching her worn cloak tighter around her body. The wind was whipping through the streets this evening and she was chilled to the bone from having to fight it. "Good night, Mr Marsh."

She made it to the stone stairs before his voice filled the night air. "How is your father, Della?"

Surprised she turned to find him right behind her. "He's well, Mr Marsh. Thank you for asking."

"Does he need anything?"

Why was Mr Marsh asking after her father? Della knew that the odious little man cared not for his prisoners on the debtor's side other than the coin that lined his pocket on behalf of the warden. "We are well, Mr Marsh," she finally decided on. The last thing she needed was to ask favours of someone that would want their own favour in return.

He nodded eagerly and Della wasted no time in entering the building and heading to their room, hoping that she would find her father well and unharmed. The sudden interest from Mr Marsh didn't bode well, not at all!

Her father was indeed in the room, unharmed and asleep and Della sagged against the doorway. She had been fearful for no reason.

But Mr Marsh's attention didn't stop with that one encounter. Della came home another time to find an additional portion of food waiting her, with Mr Marsh hovering in the hallway. "Compliments of a benefactor," was all he would say. Della had been surprised and had even coaxed her father into eating some of the extra food so it wouldn't go to waste.

What has happening, she didn't know, but as long as she wasn't propositioned for anything else, Della would take it for her father.

Even Charlotte had noted Mr Marsh's attention and commented on it when she had walked up the stairs to visit with Della.

"Perhaps you are close to paying off your debts," she mused. "It is the only reason he becomes kind to anyone."

"Nay, we cannot be," Della replied with a shake of her head. Her wages were barely covering what they were having to pay for the room, and with no benefactors, they couldn't be anywhere near close.

Unfortunately, the days turned worse as the city moved into the colder months. Her father grew despondent once more and no amount of begging could get him to eat anything. Even Ron, having come into the city for business, couldn't coerce her father into any sort of conversation.

"Father, please," she begged as she held out the cup of broth. "You need to drink this."

Her father coughed and shook his head, his cheekbones a sharp contrast to his thin face. "No, I don't want it."

Della felt the familiar sting of tears in her eyes. "But you need your strength."

"Leave me be, Della," he said, his voice weak. "I don't want anything to eat."

He turned away from her and nearly knocked the cup from Della's hands, causing her to pull it back immediately lest it ended up on the floor. Her hands shaking, she placed the cup on the desk and stared at her father's back. He had just given up on them. She had not wanted to admit it, but the evidence was there.

Her father didn't care if they starved in this prison, or that he was going to die, just like her mother had.

The tears fell unchecked and Della quickly rose from the chair, gathering her cloak as she did so. Her father didn't even make a sound as she slipped out of the room and hurried down the stairs to the prison courtyard, nearly sobbing as the cold air hit her in the face. She didn't want him to die in this prison or to end up on the other side of the prison itself!

Oh, how she wished Frederick were here right now to listen to her concerns! Her friend barely talked with her these days, as if she had offended him somehow and she missed their conversations, the laughter he brought into her otherwise dismal existence.

Her life was no different, yet it wasn't the same.

Della drew in a deep breath as she wrapped her arms around her waist and tipped her eyes to the night sky. Much of her life had been behind the bars before her, bars that kept her in and gave her no true future.

She had no future. Della didn't know exactly how much funds her father still owed nor if they were any closer to being absolved of those debts.

And what if they were? With the way her father was, Della was frightened to think about what would happen if they were turned out of the prison. While they would be free, there were no means coming in, save her wages, and her father was in no shape to contribute to supporting her. Her only options would be to stay with the Benedict household or wed.

Della suppressed a shiver. If there was a day that they would be set free, Della knew her choices would be limited. Gone was the childhood home that she had grown up in. They could appeal to her mother's family perhaps, but they hadn't come to their rescue with the letter's she had posted herself when she had become desperate.

If they were released, they would end up in East End and, given the state of her father, Della would be helpless to keep those that would hurt them at bay.

Nay, they were better here, even if she didn't want to admit it. At least there was a roof over their heads and some food in their bellies. Della would gladly sleep on the hard floor than to be pushed out into the cold streets of the city and not know what was going to befall them.

They were going to perish here. She knew it, no matter how many times she tried to find the positive in her thoughts, it came back to the very fact that Della would never make enough funds to absolve her father of his debts.

He would die and then she would be forced to become someone such as Charlotte, a woman well past her years that would eventually die, forgotten and unloved.

It wasn't the future she wished for herself or her father, but what else could they do? She was fooling herself to think that they were ever going to escape such a place.

With a sigh, Della turned to go back inside the building but as she approached the stairs, she spied Mr Marsh near the west end of the gate, his hands moving as he carried on a conversation with someone in the shadows. Mr Marsh had been unfailingly polite to her recently and Della was waiting for the moment that he would ask for something from her.

She hoped it wasn't liberties. She could never do something so… so out of her character. She wasn't that desperate.

The shadow stepped out and Della gasped as she realised who it was.

Lord Benedict, talking with Mr Marsh. Why was he here?

When had he gotten back to London? Pauline and Suzette hadn't mentioned that he was back, their discussions trailing off for the absent lord and more toward the handsome footman that had just been hired on at the household.

Della's breath caught in her throat as she realised she was staring at them and when Lord Benedict turned, she gasped once more and turned toward the stairs. She didn't know how much he knew about her being here, but the last thing she wished was to have a conversation with him in the courtyard of King's Bench for all to see.

"Della! Della, wait!"

Della closed her eyes briefly before turning toward Lord Benedict, with Mr Marsh trailing not far behind. "Lord Benedict," she stated firmly. "Whatever are you doing here?"

"Theo, please," he stated, snatching his hat off his head and crushing the brim in his hands. "I was hoping to have a word."

"With whom, my lord?" she asked.

He smiled. "With you, of course."

"Della," Mr Marsh huffed as he reached them. "Lord Benedict has been looking for you."

"And he's found me," she stated, crossing her arms over her chest. "But I'm still unclear as to why." They hadn't seen each other since that moment in the study and she had scarcely thought of him since, only the relief that she hadn't come across him.

"Della!" Mr Marsh admonished. "He is your better, girl. You will be smart to be reminded of such."

"She's not offending me," Lord Benedict said, his eyes alight with laughter. "I've enjoyed each and every meeting I've had with Della. She is far more entertaining than any other woman I've encountered."

Della looked at the two men, ignoring the earnest look in Lord Benedict's eyes. "I shouldn't be out here like this."

"Why? Mr Marsh is acting as chaperone," Lord Benedict interjected smoothly. "Isn't that correct?"

"Aye," Mr Marsh stated, crossing his arms over his chest. "I will protect your reputation, gel."

Della wasn't quite sure she believed him, but she made no move to leave.

"I have something to confess," Lord Benedict continued, placing one of his hands over his heart. "Mr Marsh has been helping me lately."

Something unfurled in Della's stomach. "Helping you with what?" She wasn't even sure how the two men knew each other.

"Learning about you," he said, his expression softening.

Della's breath stuttered in her chest. Learning about her? She was nothing more than a scullery maid in his mother's residence, one that had fallen far from where she should have been and was now working to pay off her father's debts. She was not a highborn noble any longer, nor had she ever been, in truth. Her mother, maybe, but if Lord Benedict was looking for a liaison, he wouldn't find it with Della. "Why?" she blurted out, her anxiety building as to why he was here at all. "Why would you want to learn more about me?"

"Because," Lord Benedict stated, a confident grin sliding over his lips, "I want you to be my wife."

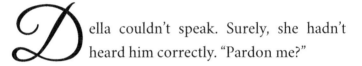ella couldn't speak. Surely, she hadn't heard him correctly. "Pardon me?"

"Della," Lord Benedict said insistently, her name rolling off his tongue as if he had said it a thousand times before. "You've bewitched me, I'm afraid."

A bubble of laughter burned in her chest, and she had to swallow hard in an effort not to laugh in his face. "Surely, this is some sort of jest," she started, looking for Lady Benedict and her friends hiding in the darkness. They would enjoy the fact that she would think this was real and genuinely believe that a gentleman, a noble at that, was asking for her hand!

"It is no jest, I swear," Lord Benedict continued, reaching out to take her hand. His leather glove was warm, as if he'd had it tucked into the pocket of his coat and Della drew in a shaky breath as he gripped it lightly. "I want you as my wife."

"B... but I'm nothing more than a servant," she responded, dumbfounded that he would even consider the thought of marrying her. What about his mother? She wasn't going to stand for it, not marrying anything more than a servant in her household. Della withdrew her hand from Lord Benedict's, feeling the loss of warmth immediately. "I'm sorry but this isn't, we can't, you can't possibly be considering."

"But I am," he interrupted, irritation coming through in his words. "And you are far more than just any servant, Della. You are a noble, by noble blood, who has fallen on hard times. There is nothing to be ashamed of what you have done for your family, but it is time for you to take your rightful place and I am pleading with you to allow that to be as my wife."

His wife. Della still felt as if she must be dreaming. His wife didn't have rough palms from the lye of the soap she used to scrub the laundry with.

His wife hadn't spent nearly her entire childhood in a prison, wearing threadbare clothing and eating food meant for the rats.

His wife wouldn't be sleeping on a pallet on the floor, waiting for the day that she was carted to a prison cell to spend the rest of her life.

His wife was someone else, and that someone wasn't her. "You can't possibly mean to go through with this," she tried again, meeting his earnest gaze. "Theo, I'm not the woman you should wed."

He didn't even flinch at her use of his Christian name. "All my life," he said instead, "I've been told how to live my life. I've been told what to wear, what school to attend, what wife I should have at my side. I've been told it is my duty to my family, but what about my duty to myself? What about what I want from my life?"

Lord Benedict's anguish was not only heartfelt, but real. Della had never seen him in such a state before, as if he were a man who had been pushed to the brink.

When he took a step closer, she didn't draw back, allowing him to take both her hands in his. "Give me a chance, Della. I can make your life, your father's life, far better than a life in this prison. You don't deserve to be here and neither does he. I can petition for an early release or find out how much he owes and pay off his debts."

At her gasp, he squeezed her hands gently. "I will do anything to make you see that I'm true in my words to you. I want to marry you."

Tears sprang in the corners of her eyes. His words sounded so genuine, the very words that she had longed to hear all her life. Was this how her mother had felt when her father had whisked her away from a fate she didn't want?

For this fate was not something that Della wished for herself or her father. She wanted to see him have the comforts of home and for her, well just to not worry so much about how they were going to continue to fight and see another day.

Could she trust him? They scarcely knew each other for him to be proposing marriage like this!

"I... I don't even know you," she replied honestly.

He leaned forward. "I will tell you whatever you wish to know. I will even ask your father properly, but I beg you, Della, don't force me to walk away without knowing that you will at least consider my offer."

Della's lips parted. It was on the tip of her tongue to deny him, to laugh at him for even thinking that she would be a good wife for him to choose.

But then she thought of her father, of how he was lying in the bed, despondent to even her. How much longer would he last in that state? Della couldn't bear to lose him. If she didn't do this for him, she would be subjecting her father to his death. She could feel it in her bones. "All right," Della heard herself say. "I will consider it."

"Take the time you need," he replied, squeezing her hands. "I would like to come by tomorrow and visit with your father and yourself."

"You want to go into the prison?" she asked, both surprised and horrified that a fine gentleman like him would see where she had been living all this time.

Lord Benedict's expression softened. "I know what you are thinking," he stated. "But I don't care, Della. You could show me a hovel in the East End, and I would still wish for you to be my wife. Nothing is going to change my mind."

His words struck a chord in her heart and Della found herself hoping that it was true, that Lord Benedict truly did wish for her to become his wife and that he actually cared for her. "You may come by tomorrow," she said, thinking that it was her only day off to catch up on their laundry and such.

"Thank you," he replied as he leaned forward. She felt the brush of his lips against her cheek and her skin prickled warmly. Perhaps this was the turning point in her life that she had been asking for, the one that was going to make all their dreams come true.

THE NEXT AFTERNOON, Della walked down the stairs, smoothing her skirts with her hands nervously. She had debated on what to wear, considering many of her things were her mother's that she had pieced together for clothing for herself. After all, she couldn't afford to purchase new clothing.

Charlotte had also given her some things over the years, outdated fashions but fine material that could be remade into skirts for her to wear when she wasn't in her servant's clothes.

That and shirts, sometimes crafted out of the finest silks, for her father. Of course, he rarely left his rooms but, today, she had told him of their visitor, and he had set himself to rights, even combing the sparse hair on top of his head in anticipation.

Della could only hope that Lord Benedict wasn't playing a trick on her and would be outside as they had discussed the previous night.

Because if he wasn't, she didn't know what she was going to do in terms of her father's morale.

Drawing in a breath, Della pushed open the door and nearly bowled Mr Marsh over in the process. "Miss Della!" he exclaimed, his cheeks ruddy from the cold wind. "I was just coming to find you."

"I'm here on time," she stated, eyeing him suspiciously. She didn't know what Lord Benedict had promised the man, but there was a reason that he had taken a liking to this sudden turn of events.

"Della, dear," Lord Benedict greeted as he rushed in, lugging a hamper on his strong arm. Della brightened as she saw the hothouse roses he held in his fist, their extravagant smell wafting in the wind. "These are for you," he said, holding them out. "Careful now, I just plucked them out of mother's conservatory this morn and I'm not certain I removed all the thorns."

"Oh, they are lovely!" Della exclaimed as she took them, not caring if they did indeed prick her fingers. Their scent, it was one from her childhood, taking her back to their own little garden when times had been easier. "Thank you, Theo, truly."

Lord Benedict flushed under her praise. "Shall we go inside? It is cold out here."

"Yes, of course," she stammered, holding open the door. Her heart thudded against her rib cage as Lord Benedict stepped inside the only home she had known for many years, the distaste on his face was not hard to miss. Perhaps to him it was dank smelling, the air clogged with coal dust, and no clean window in sight, but it was home to Della. It was home to many, having fallen on hard times either by crime or trusting the wrong person. Her memories might not all be good, but there were quite a few that were.

"This way," she continued, leading him up the stairs to the third floor, careful not to trip on her own skirts. Lord Benedict was silent the rest of the way and as they arrived at the door, she turned to him.

"You don't have to do this," Della said softly, catching his eye. "Whatever jest this is, you have taken it far enough. I shan't tell on you."

He arched a brow as he sat the hamper down on the dirty wooden floor to cup her cheek with his gloved hand. "Is that what you honestly think? That I would take the liberty of your good nature and jest with you, Della?"

Her lips parted as his thumb stroked her cheek almost lovingly, his expression full of what she could only hope as good intentions. "This is where I have lived nearly all my life," she answered, keeping the flood of tears at bay. "I'm nothing more than a daughter of a failed man."

Lord Benedict bestowed a kind smile. "You are so much more than that, Della. You are so much more than that to me. Let me prove it to you. Let me show you that I care. Let me be the one to take you from this place and put you where you belong, where both you and your father should rightfully be."

It was a dream come true, that is if it did indeed come true. "All right," she finally answered. "Then you shall meet my father."

The visit turned out to be wonderful. Her father was back to his usual charming self, asking all the appropriate questions and not once giving Lord Benedict any indication that he had been nothing more than a shell of a man previously. Della sat and watched the two men converse on various topics, her heart beginning to swell as Lord Benedict seemed to genuinely want to listen to what her father had to say. He was proving to be somewhat of a surprise to her.

What if his heart was true? What if he genuinely wanted to marry her?

The thought stayed with Della after she saw Lord Benedict out, trying not to swoon when he brushed his lips over her cheek once more. When she arrived back at their room, her father was going through the hamper, pulling items out. "There is enough food for a month in here," he stated, his eyes sparkling for the first time in a long while. "And look at this! We are saved Della! Our prayers have been answered!"

Della looked at the wad of bills in her father's hand and her heart softened once more to Lord Benedict. He could have come empty handed, yet he had brought them food and means to put a hefty sum toward her father's debt. "What did you think of him, father?" she asked as he gobbled up a fruit scone, such as she had eaten herself during Lord Benedict's visit.

Her father swallowed. "The question is, what do you think of him, daughter? He seems enamoured by you, especially so if he's willing to come inside this hell hole and meet me. That's a good judge of character in my book."

Della picked at a loose string on her skirt, contemplating all that had happened over the last two days. It seemed that Lord Benedict's promise was true, so why was she hesitating? Any other woman in her position would have already thrown herself at the gentleman, said goodbye to this dismal place, and lived the life of her dreams.

In order for her to do so, she would have to leave her father momentarily. "Father?"

His eyes found hers and they softened, much like she remembered them doing in her childhood. "Della, girl, this is right. You don't deserve to be in a place like this. Get out while you can."

"He asked me to marry him," she rushed out, the clang of dishes breaking causing them both to jump. Frederick stood in the doorway, the remains of what would have been their evening meal at his feet. His eyes were wide, and Della parted her lips, her heart in turmoil as she tried to think about what to say. "Frederick," she started but he was already turning on his heel, his clipped pace echoing down the hall.

"Let him go, daughter," her father stated, clapping his hands. "Tell me more about this engagement!"

Della let her gaze linger on the doorway before she turned her attention back to her beaming father. It was for the best. They couldn't be friends anymore once she accepted Lord Benedict's proposal.

She was going to accept the proposal.

CHAPTER 9

*T*he next few days went by in a blur. Della sent a missive through Mr Marsh that she was accepting Lord Benedict's proposal and he replied with one of his own, expressing his happiness and the need for him to inform his family with her at his side. The thought made her nauseous, so much so that she couldn't bear to work in the household she would eventually take residence in, sending around her regrets to the housekeeper that she would no longer be in employ there. It was a bold move, of course, but the funds that Lord Benedict had placed in the basket would keep them afloat for the better part of the year if somehow their engagement didn't come to pass.

Which meant she could be here for her father.

When the day came for her presentation to Lord Benedict's family, he sent around the family carriage for her, his smiling face the first thing she saw when she entered it. "I hope you don't mind," he murmured, taking in her simple grey gown. "I couldn't wait to see you."

Della blushed as she settled into the seat across from him. "Of course not." After all, they would have to learn to be in each other's company if they were to become husband and wife.

"Here," he said once the carriage started to move, holding out his hand to her. "I've brought you something."

Della gasped as she saw the large emerald ring in the palm of his hand, its stately jewel sparkling in the morning light. "That's lovely, Theo. It's far too much."

"Nothing is too much for my fiancée," Lord Benedict replied, taking her hand and placing it upon her finger. Della tried not to gawk at the ring, unable to help her thoughts on how many people it would help back at King's Bench if it were to be sold.

Nay, she wouldn't sell the ring. After today, her days would be numbered at King's Bench, along with her father's. Lord Benedict was going to ensure that their future was secure.

"Speechless my dear?" Lord Benedict asked as Della clenched her hand into a fist in fear that the ring might fall off.

"Of course, "she murmured, gazing up at him. "It is a lovely ring, Theo. I will treasure it always."

"Much like I am going to treasure your love and affection always," he finished as the carriage pulled up to the residence. "I will warn you, my dear, my mother and sister are likely to be surprised."

Della smiled. "I imagine so. It is not every day that one decides he is going to wed the hired help."

Lord Benedict's eyes widened at her cheeky remark before his chest rumbled with laughter and he threw open the door. "Come, my dear. This will be a pleasant visit."

Della hadn't graced the front entrance of the residence in the five years that she had been employed by the widow, her mouth parting as Lord

Benedict tucked her arm inside his and started up the stairs. The door opened and Della gave a small smile to the butler, Titus, who was staring back at her dumbfounded. "Miss Della," he said, his mouth rounding.

"Titus," Lord Benedict's voice boomed. "Meet my fiancée."

Titus recovered quickly, bowing to Della and she wanted to tell him to straighten himself, before stopping the words on her tongue. This would be one of the many oddities of the day, Della was certain of it. "The ladies are in the drawing room," Titus explained as he straightened, his eyes glancing at Della.

"No need to introduce us then," Lord Benedict replied, tugging on Della's arm. "Come, my dear. It is time to tell the family."

Della felt her stomach roil at the thought, but there was little time for her to plan as Lord Benedict swept into the room, startling his mother and sister. "Theo!" his mother admonished, her eyes flashing as she steadied her cup. "One of these days you are going to cause me to burn myself with my tea."

"Apologies, mother," he said dutifully, bringing Della to his side. "I've come with news."

The widow's eyes narrowed on Della. "Whatever are you doing out of uniform?" she asked as Della trembled under her glare. "What is going on here?"

"May I present my fiancée?" Lord Benedict announced.

Della saw the blood drain from the widow's face as Lady Christine gasped, nearly upsetting her own cup that was balanced on her knee. "What? This is not funny, Theo!"

"It's not a jest," Lord Benedict growled, his arm sliding from Della's and presenting her hand instead so that they could see the ring.

Lady Benedict was on her feet, faster than Della had ever seen her move before. "That is my mother's ring!"

"Given to me for my betrothed," Lord Benedict added as his mother advanced on them. "And I've chosen Della."

Della had never seen the widow so upset before and her nerves scattered as the woman grabbed her shoulders and started to shake her. "What have you done to my son you, you harlot! I knew you were up to no good, telling those stories and spreading lies! What else have you spread for him?"

"Mother!" Christine gasped, horror on her face.

Della tried to pull away from the woman's grasp, but her fingers dug into Della's bony shoulders, and she cried out. Lord Benedict stepped in and grabbed his mother's shoulders, forcing her to let go. "Mother, please! This is quite unnecessary!"

The older woman's chest was heaving in exertion. "She's bewitched you somehow, hasn't she?"

"N... no, of course not," Lord Benedict answered, pulling Della a few steps backward. "I want to marry her, and I will, with or without your blessing."

Della's heart turned over in her chest. Theo was truly standing up against his mother for her. He cared. That was the only answer.

His mother swept past them, followed by Christine and it wasn't until they were the only ones left in the room before Lord Benedict let out a breath. "That went well!"

Della turned to him. "I don't want to be the wedge between you and your mother," she stated, her heart rending in her chest as she attempted to remove the ring. She liked Lord Benedict immensely, more so after today, but she also knew how precious family was and the last thing she wanted to do was come between them.

"Della, dear," he replied, covering her hand with his and drawing her close. "She will come around. I am her only son, after all. She will remember that you are of noble blood and see that marrying you will make me happy. She just needs a little bit of time."

Della allowed Lord Benedict to draw her into the circle of his arms, breathing in his scent. Perhaps a little time would allow the widow to warm up to her.

"I want to procure you some rooms," Lord Benedict said after a few moments. "And get you out of that hellhole."

Della pulled back. "I can't possibly leave my father."

Lord Benedict's sympathetic eyes nearly caused her to tear up. "I know, but I can't get him out just yet, not until I've located all of his creditors. Give me a few days, nothing more." He cupped her cheek. "He would want you to be safe and, as my future wife, I want you to be comfortable."

"I would like to discuss it with my father first," Della said. He was her sole concern and the thought of leaving him to the prison worried her.

"Of course," Lord Benedict said. "Let's get you back then."

They traveled in silence back to the prison, but Lord Benedict didn't climb out after Della once they arrived. "I will give you a few moments to talk to him," he explained. "I have an appointment, but I will send the carriage back around to fetch you in half an hour, is that acceptable?"

Della nodded and Lord Benedict gave her a quick smile before the carriage pulled away, leaving her in front of the prison. Mr Marsh was waiting for her at the door but remained silent as she walked through. "Was that a carriage I saw you climb out of, gel?" Charlotte's voice rang out from the stairs.

Della looked up and found the older woman at the bannister. "That was Lord Benedict. He's… he's asked me to marry him."

Charlotte sniffed, clearly not impressed. "What does he want in return?"

Della's eyes grew puzzled. "My hand in marriage."

"You keep believing that, gel," Charlotte said, waving her hand at Della. "But I don't buy it for one minute. A dandy like that isn't looking for marriage."

Della didn't respond, sweeping up the stairs and knowing that Charlotte wouldn't follow her to the third floor.

"You mark my words!" the older woman called out. "You will be heartbroken and right back where you started. You hear me?"

Della continued to climb, hurrying away from the old woman's rantings. She wasn't like her. She wasn't going to give herself away without a ring on her finger and a promise that her future was secure.

Her father was waiting for her when she arrived. "Well?" he asked insistently. "How did it go?"

"It went fine," she lied. "Lord Benedict wants me to remove myself to a set of rooms he's procured for me."

"Of course, you should!" her father stated immediately, coming around to grip her shoulders. "This no place for you here, Della, girl. Not as a future lady."

Della dissolved into his arms, and he held her close. "Go on and live your life," he murmured, pressing his lips to her temple. "All I ever wanted for you was to be happy."

So, Della chose a few things to take with her, ensuring that her father had enough of the food left over from Lord Benedict's visit for the next few days. Once she was settled, she would make certain that Theo hurried along with paying off her father's debts so he could join her.

After a tearful goodbye, Della walked down the stairs, glad to see that Charlotte was nowhere to be found. As much as she loved the older woman, this was not like Charlotte's story. Della wasn't going to find herself in the same predicament.

There was, however, someone waiting for her on the first floor, coming out of the shadows of the building as Della strode to the door. "So, you are going."

Della turned to Frederick and placed her worn carpet bag on the floor. "I'm getting married, Frederick. Lord Benedict is going to pay off father's debts so I can get him out of here."

Frederick frowned. "So, you are telling me that you are going to wed someone you barely know, Della?"

She had expected this backlash from Theo's family but not from her dearest friend. "I know enough."

Frederick let out a hollow laugh, thrusting his hand through his hair. "You don't know anything about him other than you worked for his mother! What sort of man marries a servant?"

His words cut through her and Della stumbled back. "That was cruel."

The young man eyed her, regret in his eyes. "Perhaps, but it is the truth, Della. Something is amiss here. Something is not right."

"You are just jealous," she shot back, her chest aching from his hurtful words. "I thought you would be happy that I am finally getting out of this place, yet here you are, attempting to keep me in!"

"I want to get you out!" he shouted, taking a step toward her. When his large hands landed on her shoulders, Della drew in a sharp breath, the warmth coursing through her body. "I want to get you out," he repeated, his voice lowering. "You are my responsibility, Dell. Mine."

Her lips parted as she saw the earnest look on his face, a face she knew far too well. "I'm not your responsibility, Frederick," she said softly, her eyes searching his. "Not any longer."

He let out a broken laugh and released her. "You don't know, do you?" he asked, shaking his head. "I thought."

"You thought what?" she asked, unable to help herself.

His eyes met hers and Della felt his gaze all the way to her soul. "I love you, Della. I've loved you for a very long time."

Della couldn't breathe. Frederick loved her? Yes, they had become close during his time here, but love? "Frederick," she whispered.

"Tell me that you won't go," he pleaded, reaching for her. Della's breath left her lungs as she found herself against his hard chest, her hands landing on his muscular arms. "Tell me that you love me, as I do you."

When his mouth descended on hers, Della was lost. Frederick's lips were firm yet gentle as they moved over hers, as if she was made of glass.

It brought tears to her eyes.

"Please," he begged, the words whispering over her lips. "Stay with me."

Della found herself wanting to. Frederick was familiar. He knew all her secrets, her fears. Her father loved him like a son.

Her father.

Della wrenched away from him with a sob, putting some distance between them. He let his hands fall to his sides as she held her hand up to her lips. "I can't."

Hurt spread over his features but Della was already picking up her carpet bag and stumbling to the door. Thankfully the carriage was waiting, and she flung herself into it, not caring where it was taking her.

Frederick loved her. Frederick had kissed her! Why now? Why had he waited so long?

A sob tore through Della and she pressed her hand to her lips to try and muffle the sound but doing nothing for the tears streaming down her cheeks.

This was not how this day was supposed to go at all and now, instead of any happiness she would have had, there was nothing but hurt, overwhelming hurt right to her very soul.

CHAPTER 10

The carriage took her to a building near Hyde Park, a well to do area of London she had not ventured to in all her days. There was a woman waiting for her at the door, a disapproving look on her face as she took in Della's attire. "You must be Miss Gordon." She sniffed, turning on her heel without waiting for Della to respond.

The woman took her up a flight of stairs to the second level and into a light and airy room that faced the park. "Your belongings have already arrived," she stated as Della took a few steps into the room, feeling the plush carpeting under her worn leather boots.

"Belongings?" Della echoed, turning to face the woman. "What belongings?"

"Your trunks and your servants," the woman replied, handing Della an iron key. "I try to run a tight ship around here. Make certain that your door is locked when you leave, for I won't be responsible for anything that goes missing."

Before Della could ask any other questions, the door was shut, and she was left alone in the small sitting room. Drawing in a tortured breath, she looked about the room, noting the fine establishment she found herself in. While she should have been elated at the change of her rooms, no longer behind the prison gate, it was Frederick's pleading face, his declaration, that kept moving through her mind. Frederick couldn't possibly love her.

Could he?

"Oh, Miss! You are here!"

Snatched out of her thoughts, for now, Della watched as two women in maid's uniforms hurried towards her. "I'm Mollie," the shorter one replied, bobbing a polite courtesy.

"And I'm Ursula," the other stated, doing the same. "We have been hired by Lord Benedict to attend to you while you are awaiting your wedding day."

Della opened her mouth to object, but then promptly shut it. With her father in prison awaiting his release, she had no proper chaperone for the weeks ahead. It was thoughtful of Theo to already plan ahead in that regard in an effort to keep her reputation intact.

At least it wasn't his mother or sister filling that role. Della's arms still hurt from where Lady Benedict had grabbed her so roughly. "Thank you."

"Come, we were just laying out your gowns," Mollie stated, eyeing Della's worn carpet bag. "Do I need to take that?"

Della held it close to her leg, shaking her head. "No, I've got this well in hand. What gowns are you referring to?" She didn't want to tell the women that all she had was in her bag and that she was wearing the best gown she owned.

"Why, the ones in the wardrobe," Ursula replied as she moved briskly to the connecting room. Della did the same and found the large bed brimming with gowns of all different colours, along with accessories to match.

"These aren't mine," she murmured as she reached out to stroke the closest one. She hadn't possessed anything this fine since the night her family had been forced out of their home.

"Lord Benedict chose them for you," Mollie said, matter of fact, as she picked up a brilliant green that would complement the reddish hue of Della's hair. "Aren't they lovely?"

Della had to admit that they were. It seemed that Theo had thought of yet another item that Della hadn't. The extravagance of the gowns on the bed could easily feed those at King's Bench for months alone.

Forcing herself to push aside those thoughts, she snatched her hand back. The last thing she wished to do was put the filth of the prison, of the home she had known for years, on the material. "I think I would like to take a bath." After years of bathing in a basin, Della longed to have a proper bath.

"Of course!" Mollie exclaimed as Della sat her bag on the seat at the foot of the bed. "I will run one for you straight away."

"And I shall find you a long chemise," Ursula stated as she started to place the gowns back into the wardrobe. "Dinner will be sent up shortly."

Della didn't respond, watching the two of them as they worked to please her. When was the last time she hadn't had to lift a finger to help herself? She knew every aching movement of their tasks and how odd it felt to be watching from the outside, looking in, now. Della wanted to help. She wanted to do more than just stand there and watch them work.

Yet there was an odd weight lifted off her shoulders at the thought of Lord Benedict bringing her father to a place like this after his debts were paid. Better yet, he could stay with them at their official residence.

Where would that be? Would they remain in London? Della suddenly had far too many questions for her new fiancé than she had answers. The first concern was that his family was clearly against the marriage. It pained her, even if it didn't Theo, to have his mother not bless their union. Perhaps she had to warm up to the idea. After all, Della could hardly blame her for wondering if her son was making the right decision.

"Miss Gordon? Your bath is ready."

"Thank you," Della replied. "And please call me Della."

Mollie's eyes rounded. "Oh, I couldn't possibly!"

"Please," Della insisted, giving her a warm smile. "Because just yesterday I was wearing a uniform like yours."

The two women exchanged looks. "Alright," Mollie finally said, giving her a small smile in return. "I will attempt to do so."

"Good," Della answered. "I can undress myself if you would like to look out for my dinner."

"Of course, Miss," Ursula said, placing the last dress in the wardrobe. She had already laid out a nightgown of fine silky lawn, one that was embroidered with tiny rosebuds that made Della smile. "We will be right outside, Miss."

Della watched as the two maids walked out of the connecting room and slid the panel doors closed, leaving Della with her own thoughts. She didn't remain there for long. Della walked into the bathing chamber and tears pricked her eyes as she saw the

steaming bath awaiting her. It was as if she had just
stepped into someone else's life.

TWO DAYS PASSED before Della decided she couldn't
sit around any longer. Lord Benedict had sent
missives to her that he was tied up with business
dealings and Della wanted to check in on her father
to ensure that he was well without her constant
watch. But the moment she mentioned to her maids
that she would like to bring a hackney around to do
so, they exchanged looks. "We can't let you do that,
Miss Gordon," Mollie spoke up, her voice laced with
sympathy.

"Why not?" Della asked, arching a brow. "If it's
funds."

"It's not funds," Ursula said quickly, glancing at
Mollie. "It is Lord Benedict's request that he take you
to the prison. After all, it is a dangerous place for
someone of your station, now."

Her station? Della looked down at the cream-
coloured gown she had put on that morning. She
wasn't wed to Theo yet and, until he absolved her
father of his debts, she was still a ward of King's

Bench. "I must insist," she said firmly, lifting her chin. "I need to see my father."

"I will send a missive to Lord Benedict," Mollie replied, rushing to the writing desk. As she did so, Della moved toward the door of the sitting room, opening it, only to find a footman standing outside, his eyes fixed on hers. "Miss Gordon?" he asked politely. "Are you in need of something?"

"N… no," Della responded, shutting the door before he could say anything else. Had she traded one prison for another?

It didn't take long for Lord Benedict to arrive that afternoon once the missive was sent, sweeping into the sitting room with a broad smile on his face. "My darling," he announced, gathering Della's hands and placing a chaste kiss on them. "I hear you wish to visit your father."

"I do," Della murmured. "And based on your instructions, I'm not allowed."

Lord Benedict squeezed her hands lightly. "Of course not! That wasn't my intent." He gave her a warm smile. "My intent is to keep you safe, Della. It is no place for my fiancé to go alone."

Some of Della's anger lessened. "I miss him," she said honestly. "I would like to see him."

"And you shall," Frederick said tenderly. "Because we have wonderful news to share with him."

"What's that?" Della asked, surprised.

Frederick's smile grew wider, and he kissed her hands again before releasing them. "Why, the first banns have been read on our upcoming marriage, my dear. We are to be wed two weeks from today!"

Two weeks? Della's lips parted. "I can see the shock in your eyes, my dear," Frederick continued. "But, alas, I can't wait to have you as my wife. I hope that is suitable for you."

Was it suitable? Della thought about objecting but then again, what was she waiting on? The sooner she became Lady Benedict, the faster she could urge her husband to get her father out of King's Bench and start a new life. Every moment was crucial now. "Of course, it is," she finally said, pasting on a smile. "I can't wait either."

Frederick's smile was breathtaking. "Then it's settled! Get my fiancée's wrap. We are going to visit her father."

Della's heart was light as they rode to the prison, eager to ensure that her father was being cared for properly. Mollie rode with them for propriety's sake but gazed out of the window while Theo held Della's hand and brushed his lips over her cheek, causing her to shiver against his intimate touch. Soon they wouldn't need a chaperone and, while the thought should have filled her with anticipation, the closer they got to King's Bench, the more she thought of another gentleman in her life.

Lord Benedict escorted her up the stairs and once they reached the room, Della felt some anxiousness ease as she saw her father sitting up in the bed, a wan smile on his face. He was starting to look worse, and she knew she had to get him out of this place before it was too late. "Della, girl," he said hoarsely. "Look at you. You look like your mother."

Della smiled and clasped his bony hand in hers. "Theo is working on getting your debts paid. Soon you will be able to leave, father."

"Yes," Lord Benedict added, his hand possessively on Della's shoulder. "We are to be wed in two weeks' time. I hope to have you out of here by then so you may give your daughter away at her wedding."

"Two weeks? What's the rush?"

The couple turned to find Frederick in the doorway, a scowl on his face as he gazed at Lord Benedict. He was holding a tray, the steam from the broth visible in the cold room. "Frederick," Della said softly, stepping forward and away from Lord Benedict's touch.

He didn't answer her, instead setting the tray on the desk. "I tried to get you an extra helping tonight, sir."

"Aye, you are a good boy," her father replied weakly.

Della turned to Lord Benedict, placing her hand on his arm. "Theo, I thought someone was going to take care of my father for me. Surely he can get more than just a bowl of broth."

Lord Benedict patted her hand with his. "Of course, my darling. I will see to it at once, but we must be going. I wish to have dinner with you this evening."

Della bit her lip as she looked at her father, who nodded. "Go on, Della, girl. You are far too fancy for the likes of this place now."

"Yes, Della," Frederick chimed in. "There's no need for you to be here."

His words stung, but she didn't let him see the devastation in her eyes, leaning over to kiss her father's paper-thin cheek instead. "It shan't be long father. I promise."

"I will see that Mr Marsh brings up another tray of food," Lord Benedict cut in as Della pulled away. "And ensures he eats every morsel."

Della gave him a grateful smile, ignoring Frederick as Lord Benedict said his goodbyes and they walked out of the room, her hand tucked in the crook of her fiancé's arm. It was better this way, this bout of anger with Frederick. He didn't know what she was trying to do for her father, what she was trying to do for their future.

He wouldn't understand, and if she lost a friend in the process, then so be it. Her father was everything to her, the only family she had left, and she must get him out of King's Bench before it took him away from her.

CHAPTER 11

*T*he next week flew past like a cold winter's wind. Della found herself thrown into the planning of her own wedding, spearheaded by her fiancé and his mother. Lady Benedict finally came to visit Della after she had been in her rooms for five days, begrudgingly admitting to the fact that her son was going to marry a former house servant and declaring that the wedding had to be the best one London had seen in order to overcome that slight blunder.

Della's head was soon filled with names she had never heard of, foods and décor that she could only murmur in agreement to, and a church she had never set foot in. "All the well to do from London society marry there," Lady Benedict had replied when Della had attempted to ask a question. "You don't understand how hard we must work toward ensuring that they accept you, my dear. My son is a pillar of society and now that you are to be his wife, you will have to overcome the fact that you were once a maid."

Della was at least grateful that her future mother-in-law didn't know where Della had spent her youth, for she would likely have had an apoplectic fit if she knew her precious son was marrying not only a servant but one that had been housed in debtor's prison at that!

Lord Benedict came by often during the days leading up to the wedding, escorting Della to drawing rooms of his mother's friends, well placed invites that would benefit her in the upcoming season. She smiled and laughed, showed off her ring and discussing her wedding details, but Della didn't find joy in any of it.

She tried. Oh, she tried to find the acceptance that this was going to be her life as Lady Benedict, that these people would accept her eventually, but she wasn't remiss at the fluttering of their fans while they whispered behind her back, or how shrewd her soon to be mother-in-law's eyes grew when Della forgot some society rule.

What was wrong with her? Della drew in a breath as she waited for Lady Christine to arrive for tea, picking at the lace on the skirts of her fine gown. Something was missing in her life, something that she had grown rather fond of. It was the nature of her friendship with Charlotte, or how Frederick would make her laugh when she was feeling poorly.

It was the way her father's eyes lit up when Ron visited, or how she had laughed with the servants from the very household she was about to be part of. All her life Della thought that if she could just remove herself from the situation that had befallen her family, that she would be happy but now that she was far removed from it, there was no happiness.

Only, well, apprehension. Even a bit of dread.

It was not how a bride was supposed to be three days before her wedding.

The door opened and Lady Christine swept in, garishly dressed in a yellow gown that did nothing for her complexion. "Dear Lady Christine," Della murmured as the woman took her place across from her. "May I interest you in a cup of tea?"

"Of course," Christine replied, her eyes darting to the maids that hovered nearby. "You are looking well. Do you feel well, Della?"

Della carefully poured the tea from the pot. "Whatever do you mean?"

"Nothing," Lady Christine snapped. "I am just asking after your welfare, of course. Am I not allowed to do so?"

Della set the pot down, surprised by Christine's outburst. "Forgive me. I didn't mean to offend you." If she were going to find some glimmer of hope in this marriage, she could ill afford to make an enemy of her future sister-in-law.

Christine sniffed as she picked up her teacup. Della did the same, but Christine's somehow slipped, and the scalding tea wound up in her lap instead. "Oh!" Della cried out, setting her own teacup down quickly so she could pick up something to blot the liquid with.

Her maids came forward, but Christine flung out her hand, halting them in their place. "Stop! Only Della will attend to me in the bedroom."

"M… milady, "Mollie stammered as Christine stood, tea running down the length of her gown. "Please."

"Della," Christine said sharply. "I shall require a steady hand to change."

Finding it odd, Della walked with the woman to the bedroom, watching as the woman slid the doors shut. "I have many gowns you can choose from," Della said, starting toward the wardrobe. "Though they might be a tad short for you."

Christine grabbed her arm and held her fingers to her lips, motioning that they move to the bathing chamber instead. Only once Della was pressed against the tub, a bit frightened, did the woman speak. "I don't have long," she explained in a hushed tone, her eyes darting toward the closed door of the bathing chamber. "Those women have been instructed not to leave you alone with anyone but, luckily for you, they are afraid of me."

The other woman smiled, and Della didn't know what to think. "You must leave here at the first opportunity," Christine continued. "Before the wedding."

"What?" Della asked, completely shocked at what she was hearing. Leave?

"Don't ask questions," Christine urged. "Just listen. I can't tell you what is going on, but it is in your best interests to leave." Some of her bravado faltered and for a moment, Della thought she saw true concern in the woman's eyes. "Your father..."

"Miss Gordon? Lady Benedict?"

"Drat," Christine muttered, reaching for the buttons on her bodice. "Quickly now, they will open that door at any moment."

Della's fingers fumbled at the other woman's buttons at her back, succeeding in getting the gown loose as her mind whirled with this turn of events. What was it that Christine was about to say about her father?

Why must she leave?

The door opened suddenly, and Christine gasped, holding her now freed dress in her hands over her bosom. "How dare you!" she admonished the red-faced maids. "Can't a lady have any sort of privacy? I will report you to my brother for this!"

The maids scurried from the door and Christine winked at Della. "Good luck."

Della was still attempting to figure out the mystery when Lord Benedict visited later that evening to dine with her, as he had done every night since they had visited the prison. "You look perturbed, my dear," he said as Della picked at her food. "Did something happen today?"

"N... no, of course not," Della replied, deciding that until she could figure out Christine's true motives, that she should keep the odd visit to herself. "I'm just a bit nervous about the wedding."

He smiled, reaching across the table to grasp her free hand. "It is understandable. You are about to become Lady Benedict.

She gave him a wan smile. "How is it progressing with getting my father out of King's Bench, Theo?"

Her fiancé removed his hand, his smile turning downward. "It's proving to be harder than I thought. Your father owed a great deal of money to many people, my darling."

"But you are Lord Benedict," she insisted, the first sliver of doubt creeping into her mind. "Surely, you have some influence."

"Not enough," Lord Benedict replied, nodding to her barely touched meal. "Eat up, my darling. You'll need your strength to deal with my mother in the days ahead."

"I want to go and see him," Della decided after a few moments. "I would like to go and see him, Theo."

"No," Lord Benedict said briskly as he sawed into his roast with a silver knife. "I will endeavour to get him to our wedding day, but I will not take you back to that place again, Della. It is unsafe for you."

A bubble of laughter welled up in her throat and she had to force it back down. Unsafe? She of all people knew how safe it truly was. "Please, Theo," she tried once more, reaching over to touch his arm. "I just need to ensure he's well."

Lord Benedict's gaze darkened as he glared at her. "I said no, Della, and that is final. Do not push me on this."

Della removed her hand as if he had bitten it, ire raising in her veins. He had never spoke to her like that before, never denied her any request.

She fell silent the rest of the meal and when Theo went to leave for the night, he pulled her close as he always did, staring into her eyes. "Do not be cross with me, darling," he murmured, his hand tightening on her waist. "I only wish to protect you from that place."

"Of course," she whispered, allowing him to brush his lips over hers before he left the room. For a moment she stood there, her chest heaving, not in sadness but anger.

"Miss?" Mollie asked hesitantly from the corner. "Would you like for me to draw you a bath?"

Della allowed the glimmer of tears to shine in her eyes. "No, thank you. I think I will retire for the night."

The maids exchanged looks but Della was already moving to the bedroom, waiting until she had slid the doors closed before she blinked away the tears. Christine had been right. She needed to get out of this place and fast. Something wasn't right.

There was no way she could wed Lord Benedict now.

Della waited a few moments, faking her sobs so that the maids could hear them on the other side of the doors before she moved silently to the wardrobe, stripping off the lovely blue gown she had slipped on for her fiancé this evening.

Her hands slid over the silken fabrics of the gowns before she found her old one, stuffed in the back so that the maids wouldn't burn it. With trembling hands, Della stepped into the familiar clothing, adding a layer of woollen stockings from her valise on her legs. It was bitterly cold outside and if she were to climb out of the window, she would need the extra protection.

Yes, she was going to climb out of the window. The good news was that she was only on the second floor of the building, and each window had a rather large ledge under it. If she could get out of the window and onto the ledge, then it was just a small drop to the ground below, a ground that would be softened by the snow that lay over it.

Della wasted no time winding the scarf around her neck and throwing on her old coat and gloves before replacing the slippers with her old boots. In this clothing, she felt more like herself, more like Della Gordon.

The window sash slid up easily and Della looked back at the cozy room before she climbed through the open window, her hands nearly slipping on the icy ledge. The ledge was a bit narrower than she had originally thought and her breath halted in her lungs as she fought to gain her balance lest she fall off without controlling her fall. Once she was steady, Della looked up. Dusk was falling over London, which meant she had less than an hour to get to the prison before it closed for the night.

Once Della nudged the window nearly closed, she peered over the ledge on all fours, a bit dizzy from the height. This was going to work. She was going to make it and without injury.

Her father was counting on her.

Drawing in a breath, Della lowered herself until she was sitting on the ledge and used her hands to push away without thinking about it any longer, feeling the ledge disappear under her grip and then she was falling to the ground.

CHAPTER 12

*A*t first Della felt weightless, the ground hurtling toward her at an alarming speed that she had no time to cry out. The snow drift was at least as deep as she had thought and she fell into it, the cold seeping into her clothing but sustaining no other injury.

She wasted no time in scrambling out of the snow drift and running unladylike down the sidewalk, keeping an eye on the sky. The wind tore at the damp clothing, but Della paid it no heed. She could survive a bit of cold if it meant she could save her father.

It made no sense for Theo to deny her admittance to see her father. He had promised that he would look after her father, get him out of his debts so that he could be free like Della was.

Now, she wasn't so certain that had been Lord Benedict's plan at all. Whatever his plan was, it wasn't for the sake of the future that she wished to have with her family.

As much as the tears wanted to flow from her eyes, Della held them in. She had thought that Lord Benedict was the answer to their prayers, the saviour who was going to give them both a future, one that they deserved.

He was proving not to be any of those things, though Della wasn't certain what his true motives were.

When the prison came into view, Della nearly cried out in relief, seeing that the gate was still open, but there was a man standing at the gate, his hand poised to swing it closed. "Stop!" she called out. "Please!"

The man halted and she realised it was Mr Morris. "Della?" he asked, squinting in the dying light. "Whatever are you doing here?"

"Please," she gasped, the words coming out in a pant more than a plea. "I must see my father, immediately."

Mr Morris frowned. "Why ever would you want to come back in?"

"You can lock me in for the evening," she tried again. "Please." She just needed to ensure that he was safe.

Mr Morris opened the gate. "Come on then. Quickly."

She gave him a grateful smile as she slipped through the opening that he provided and headed to the stairs, her heart thudding in her chest. Della wasted no time climbing the three flights of stairs to the landing and hurrying down the hall toward her father's room. Charlotte was just coming out of the room when Della reached it, her eyes wide. "What are you doing here, gel?"

"My father," she rasped. "Please tell me that he's well."

Charlotte's gaze narrowed. "You shouldn't be here, Della."

Della pushed past the older woman and gasped as she caught a glimpse of her father lying on the bed, the smell of vomit and refuse heavy in the air. "Father!" she cried as she collapsed at his bedside.

How had this happened?

"He's been sick for days," Charlotte murmured as she lowered herself into the chair near Della. "He can't keep anything in his stomach, not even a drop of water."

Della pushed past the shock and grief of seeing her father in such a state and picked up his hand, finding it cool to the touch. "We need to keep him warm," she said, emotion clogging her throat. Oh, how she wished she had brought some coal or the large blanket on the bed from the suite!

"I've used up just about all my coal," Charlotte replied with a sigh as Della tucked the blankets that were piled upon him tightly around his body to ward off the chill of the room.

Della looked over at the old woman, her lips parting in surprise. "You've been taking care of him?" Charlotte hadn't been a staunch supporter of Thomas Gordon and how he wasn't doing anything to better their lives, instead allowing Della to take up the work.

Charlotte gave a little shrug. "Who else was going to do so? You were gone, off gallivanting with your lord and Frederick, that boy up and disappeared days ago. What else was I supposed to do?"

Frederick was gone? Della swallowed hard, a tightness curling in her chest. There were a few things she would like to say to him, things that perhaps she should have listened to the day he told her he loved her. With Theo, he had been everything she had needed, everything that her father had needed, yet now she was here, with nothing.

She could lose the most important person in her life. "You were right," Della said softly. "About Lord Benedict."

Charlotte sighed. "I figured as much. What was it? Was it your peerage that finally ruined it or his wandering eye?"

"He refused to let me come see my father," she stated, her eyes straying to her father's pale face. "He told me he was going to pay off his debts and he would be there for the wedding, but I'm not certain if that was ever his plan at all."

Charlotte reached over and laid her hand on Della's shoulder, squeezing it gently. "Well, it doesn't matter now. You are here. That's all that he's going to care about in the end."

Della didn't want to think about this being her father's final days. She had been young when her mother had passed, but old enough to understand what was happening. To lose her father would be a harsh blow that Della wasn't sure she would ever recover from. Now that she had no future with Lord Benedict, she also didn't want to think about what would become of her. The only thing of value she had was her engagement ring, which would be sold at the first opportunity if her father made it through the night, to get him some help.

"I don't know what to do," Charlotte continued, dropping her hand. "He's just wasting away before our eyes."

Della didn't know what to do either. No physician was going to pay a call to the prison. The warden would never allow it and since she had all but begged Mr Morris to lock her inside, Della couldn't possibly get out tonight to find one.

Wiping the tears from her eyes, Della forced herself to stand. Well, she wasn't about to give up just yet, not while her father's chest still rose and fell. "Food," she stated, stripping off her old coat and draping it over his still form. "What about his food?"

"He's not going to keep it down," Charlotte grumbled as she pushed herself out of the chair. "But I will go and find Mr Marsh, if you insist."

Della reached out and pulled the older woman into an embrace. "Thank you, Charlotte. I know I didn't listen to you, yet you still watched out for him. I... I'm sorry, I was too stubborn."

"Hush, gel," Charlotte said, though her arms embraced Della quickly. "You remind me of myself at times but more importantly, of the daughter I was never able to have."

Surprised, Della pulled back to find tears in the stubborn woman's eyes. "I would have been honoured to be your daughter."

Charlotte sniffed as she released Della, wiping at her eyes. "I will see to that tray."

Della didn't turn back to her father until the room was empty, sitting gently on the bed. "Father, please," she said, grasping his hand and pressing her lips to the back of it. "Please, don't leave me. I need you so much."

To her surprise, her father's eyes fluttered at the sound of her voice, focusing until they found her.

"What are you doing here?" he rasped, his eyes widening. "You can't be here! No, not my daughter!"

"Whatever are you talking about father?" Della asked, alarmed that he would react in such a manner. "Of course, I would be here. I'm not leaving again."

"No, no," he moaned, attempting to pull his hand away from her, "he said you would be protected. He said you wouldn't fall ill."

"I'm not ill," she rushed to tell him. "You are, and now that I am here, I'm going to get you some help." It broke her heart to see him like this, left to think that she may fall ill if she had stayed.

"You're not sick?" he asked.

Della shook her head, giving him a small smile. "I'm not sick."

Her father's eyes darkened. "He lied to me. He kept you away."

He dissolved into a coughing fit and Della hurriedly reached for the glass of tepid water on the desk to help him. "Who lied to you?" she asked when he quieted, his head back on his pillow. Della felt as if she already knew the answer to her question, but she needed to hear it from his lips.

"Lord Benedict," her father replied quietly.

Della closed her eyes briefly against the onslaught of emotions that slammed into her. What else had Theo done? He had lied to her father, attempted to keep Della away from him for what? Up until now, she had readily accepted that she was going to wed him.

Footsteps at the door caught her attention and she watched as Mr Marsh walked in with a tray, Charlotte right behind him. "I found him," the older woman replied as the tray was placed on the bed. "Ah, you're awake. Good. You can eat something."

Della helped her father sit up in bed, feeling the bones at his back as she did so. "I don't think I'm going to be able to keep it down," her father said, as he panted, sweat breaking out on his forehead as Della lifted the tray."

"You should try to," Mr Marsh said nervously, his hands behind his back. "It is bad for business to lose a prisoner on this side of the wall."

Della shot him a glare as she picked up the spoon, stirring the cloudy broth. The steam felt good on her cool face, and she wished that she could just eat it herself. Having not eaten much at dinner it was starting to catch up with her and her stomach grumbled at the smell of the broth.

Instead, she put on a smile as she picked up the bowl. "I want you to eat all of it," she told her father, placing it in his trembling hands. "Or else you will not get your sweets."

He smiled at her and her heart broke. "That was something your mother used to say."

Della nodded. "And she would be right here, carrying on as I have been, as well. I know you miss her, but I need you, father. I need you a great deal." Della was frightened about the prospect of losing him too.

He set his chin as he lifted the broth to his mouth. "Then I will attempt to keep this down."

There was the sound of running in the hall that drew their attention and Della gasped as Frederick barrelled through the door, his eyes widening as he saw them. "No!" he shouted, knocking the bowl askew.

"Frederick!" Della cried out, barely missing the splash of the hot liquid as it soaked the items on the desk. "Whatever are you doing? Father needs that food!" Now, she would have to appeal to Mr Marsh to bring a fresh tray.

But as she looked for him, she found the little man nowhere in sight. Instead, Ron was standing at the doorway, his chest heaving. "Are we too late?"

"Too late for what?" Della asked, thoroughly confused.

"What is the meaning of this?" Charlotte demanded, tapping her cane on the wood floor.

Della glared at Frederick, who was staring at her father as if he hadn't seen him for days. According to Charlotte he hadn't. "I thought we were too late," he said softly, thrusting a hand through his hair. "I thought…"

The entire situation wasn't making any sense. Reaching up, Della grabbed Frederick's shoulders and forced him to meet her angry gaze. "Tell me what is going on right now or heaven help me I will let Charlotte beat it out of you!"

CHAPTER 13

"The food was poisoned," Frederick replied, his jaw working. "They were trying to kill your father."

Della couldn't believe what she was hearing. "But why?" she asked, pushing her fingers into his shoulders. "Why would anyone want to kill him?"

Ron stepped in as Frederick gently removed her hands from his shoulders, clasping one of them in his. Della drew from his warmth, deciding that she would also need his strength for the tale that was about to be told and laced their fingers together. She felt Frederick's start of surprise, but he didn't attempt to pull away from her.

If nothing else, the hand tightened on hers.

"Because, lass," Ron was saying, "he is about to inherit a goodly sum of money."

"What?" her father barked out; his voice stronger than it ever had been. "I have no funds. Inherit? My parents are long since dead and there were no other siblings."

"Not from your family," Frederick interjected, his eyes on Della, "but from your mother's."

"My mother?" she whispered. "But her family disowned her. How would you have come across that information?"

"I've been doing some discreet digging on yer behalf," Ron stated, his bushy eyebrows raising ever so slightly. "Ye needed help and I figured if I could appeal tae yer mother's side, then maybe they would send some funds."

"Which is when Ron found out that they were all deceased," Frederick supplied.

"So, I asked around the village about relatives and such," Ron continued, picking up where Frederick had left off. "And it seems that they had a solicitor in London."

"I visited the solicitor this afternoon," Frederick said, his eyes flickering to Della's father. "And you are the sole heir to the entire fortune. It is enough to pay off your debts a hundred times over."

The blood drained from Thomas's face. "You're jesting," he whispered. "They detested me. They would never have left me a solitary farthing."

"They didn't," Ron spoke up. "They left it to their daughter and whatever family she possessed."

"Which is where you come in," Frederick said softly, squeezing Della's hand. "With your father gone, you stood to inherit it all."

"I still don't understand," Della said, shaking her head. "What does that have to do with the poisoning? Who would wish that on my father?" The moment the words were out of her mouth, Della gasped, pressing the back of her hand to her lips.

Theo. That was why he didn't want her to see her father like this! She would know something was wrong and demand that he be taken care of.

"He found out about the money, didn't he?" she whispered, sick to her stomach.

Frederick's solemn expression told her all that she needed to know. "I can't confirm it," he told her, rubbing his thumb over her knuckles. "But Lord Benedict was at the solicitor's office as early as this morning inquiring about the money. He's put the pieces together, Dell. He knows he will be an even richer man when he marries you, with funds to do as he likes."

"And kills off yer father," Ron added. "Which we were just in the nick of time tae stop."

Della turned to her father, flushing as he was eyeing the tightly clasped hands between her and Frederick. "How long has Mr Marsh been bringing your food?" she asked.

"Weeks now," Charlotte spoke up. "Since you left, I suppose. I've found him in here, helping him eat and such but just thought that your fiancé had put him to watching out for your father, not killing him."

Della's knees nearly gave out, causing Frederick to place his arm around her waist to steady her. "Easy now," he said softly into her ear. "I've got you."

"I don't believe this," her father seethed, red taking over the paleness of his face. "I don't mind so much about my dying, but they have used my daughter and that is unacceptable!"

"What do we do now?" Della asked, pulling away from Frederick and looking over his shoulder at Ron. "If Mr Marsh is behind this, Lord Benedict might already know."

"We need the solicitors," her father replied. "Rouse them from their beds! We will not be denied what is rightfully ours!"

"Father, please," Della urged. "You are in no condition to handle this matter, and certainly not tonight. We will go first thing in the morning." She looked at Frederick and Ron. "We can go at first light and beat Lord Benedict at his own game."

"He's going tae know aboot yer father," Ron reminded her. "He's not safe here."

"Perhaps not," Della decided, tugging on the ring that was on her finger, the very one she had looked at so longingly a few short weeks ago. "But the warden might be swayed to allow us out."

IN THE END, her bribe worked. The warden took the ring as a promise of payment, mainly because it was worth more than what her father still owed, and they were allowed to leave the prison under certain conditions. Though it was difficult, Ron and Frederick got her father down the stairs in his weakened state and to the waiting coach, Della in tow. Charlotte had elected to stay behind and keep watch on Mr Marsh's whereabouts, though Della knew that once they settled this matter, she would also be getting the older woman out of the prison as well.

Ron was able to procure a set of rooms away far from the ones that Della had escaped from and, once her father was settled in, Della met with both Ron and Frederick about the plans for the next morning. "I will bring the solicitor's around first thing," Ron replied. "Thomas is in no condition tae be traveling until he's gained some of his strength back."

"I agree," Frederick stated, his jaw clenched. "I think that we need to ensure the inheritance is secure and then we deal with Lord Benedict."

Della would like to deal with her ex-fiancé as well, but it would be on her terms. "I will work out a plan," she stated, thinking of one ally she had in the Benedict household.

"He will be desperate to find you," Frederick added. "He can't inherit anything unless you marry him."

Della rose from the settee and found some paper in the desk. "I have a plan," she said, pursing her lips. She quickly wrote a missive and handed it to Frederick, who grinned as he read it. "Are you certain you want to do this?" he asked.

Della clasped her hands behind her back, smiling. "Of course. If the warden thinks my father has died, then Mr Marsh will as well. He saw the state that my father was in. He knows that he's weak and likely wouldn't survive the journey. That way Lord Benedict will think that he has won."

"But ye aren't in his grasp any longer," Ron added with a frown.

"The banns are read," Della replied. "The wedding is to take place two days from now. It would be nothing for him to forge my signature on the certificate and present that to the solicitors." If he were as cunning as she thought, Lord Benedict wouldn't let the setback of her not being in his grasp hold him from such wealth. He would just simply find a way around it. "He will feign that I am sick or grieving over my father's death to explain my absence."

"Then you plan to do what?" Frederick prodded.

"I will meet him at the solicitor's office," she answered with a grim smile on her face at the thought of seeing him once more. "He won't do anything until he's received the missive that my father is dead. I'm certain of it." Besides, Lord Benedict wasn't going to be the one to explain to his mother or his sister that Della wasn't going to be attending the grand wedding in two days. She suspected he would already have left the country.

"Well, then," Ron said, pushing up from the chair. "I will deliver the missive. I've placed some trusted men in the hallway tonight. Ye and Thomas will rest easy."

"Thank you, Ron," Della breathed, tears sparkling at her eyes. Never again was she going to have to worry about their safety or their livelihood.

He nodded and after giving Frederick a look, disappeared through the doorway.

"I must go as well," Frederick replied once they were alone in the sitting room. "It is not appropriate for me to be here with you."

"Thank you, Frederick," she said softly. "I'm sorry."

Frederick shook his head, taking her hand in his. "Don't apologise. It wasn't right for me to say what I did when you had just accepted another man's proposal. I was jealous and angry."

Della's heart tumbled in her chest. "Do you... do you not love me then?"

He reached up and tucked her hair behind her ear, something he had done for as many years as she had known him. "Of course, I love you," he said, his eyes searching hers. "I've loved you for such a long time, Della. Perhaps if I had told you long ago, you wouldn't be in this predicament now."

Della cupped his cheek with her hand. "If you had, I might not believe it as much as I do now."

Frederick smiled and she felt a lightness about her that hadn't been there before. "Perhaps you could love me as well, one day?" he asked softly. "Because I will wait for you until the end of my days, Dell."

"Oh Frederick," she sighed, the words tumbling out. "I think I'm already halfway there."

When he leaned down this time, there was no anger to his kiss, just the light brushing of his lips over hers. "Then I shall hold you to that, Della Gordon."

Della watched him go, wrapping her arms around her waist and smiling to herself. She truly hoped that Frederick did because he was her future.

WHEN DELLA WALKED into the solicitor's office that afternoon, she wasn't alone. Frederick was there of course, but there was a new addition to her small family, one that was giddy with excitement.

She could also tell the moment that Lord Benedict realized he had been duped. "What is the meaning of this!" he said angrily, rising from the chair as Della walked through the door. "Della, darling?"

"Don't darling me," she stated angrily. "You are trying to steal my family's fortune."

Lord Benedict's expression was one of shock, but the hardness in his eyes was impossible to miss. "I know you are grieving the loss of your father, my dear," he said gently. "I was just explaining to your solicitor that we wed quickly last evening so that he could be there."

"It is funny you should say that, Lord Benedict," the solicitor stated, taking his spectacles off to wipe them on his sleeve. "For I spoke with Mr Gordon this morning and he seems to be in fine health. In fact, it's quite a miracle."

"A miracle you didn't anticipate," his sister, Lady Christine replied. When Della had sent the missive to her, she hadn't expected the woman to agree so readily. After all, this was her brother, her flesh and blood that they would be duping.

But the older woman had gleefully agreed, and Della couldn't help but wonder if she had just gained a new friend.

"Christine," Lord Benedict stated, his jaw ticking. "Whatever are you doing here?"

"I'm here to tell you that mother knows everything you have done," she answered, causing him to pale. "And she's rightly upset with you, something about cutting off any remaining funds of hers and sending you to the colonies to fend for yourself. That is, if these nice people aren't going to press charges."

"I think that we have had enough of prison for one lifetime," Della replied. She and her father had discussed with the solicitor regarding what Lord Benedict's punishment should be, and as much as she wanted to see him enjoy the cell or worse, she just wanted him out of their lives. "I am willing to barter for your freedom, Theo. You can leave today for the colonies, escorted to the ship by one of my father's companions and I will not go to the police."

"And if I refuse?" he asked tightly.

"Then I will go to the police," she finished. "I've spent nearly all my life inside a prison. I've made a few friends along the way, and they will see that you are in a cell, not in debtor's prison, for attempting to kill my father."

Lord Benedict sputtered but the damage was done, and he swept his hat off the chair, jamming it on his head. "It seems that I need to speak to mother."

"She will have you arrested on the spot," Lady Christine added gleefully. "She said you are no longer welcome at our home or country estate. This is your only option, brother."

Della stepped aside and Ron walked up. "Come, Lord Benedict," he said, grabbing him by the upper arm. "I will ensure that ye donna miss yer boat."

Once Lord Benedict was gone, Della let out a ragged sigh. "Thank you," she said to Christine, hugging the older woman. "I know it was hard."

Lady Christine laughed. "Not as hard as you think, truly. I've been trying to get rid of him for years. He is a scoundrel and always has been."

Della decided she didn't want to know any more of Christine's devious thoughts and, after she promised to come for tea, Lady Christine left as well.

"Well, Miss Gordon," the solicitor replied, leaning back in his chair. "I can honestly tell you that this is the most entertainment I have had in many a year. Are you ready to begin a new life?"

Della looked at Frederick, who gave her a smile that held the promise of a future that she had always dreamed of. "I do believe so."

After gathering the packet of papers detailing all her father's new assets, Della and Frederick walked out into the brilliant sunshine. "Charlotte isn't going to be happy moving out of the prison," Frederick replied. "She will miss it."

Della laughed. "I'm sure she will enjoy the wilds of Scotland." The older woman was part of her family now, and Della couldn't possibly leave her behind.

"Scotland?" Frederick asked as he proffered his arm to her.

"I apparently have a large manor there," Della replied, sliding her arm into his and resting her hand on his strong forearm. "What do you think about living the life of a Scottish Laird?"

Frederick paused on the pavement, bringing Della around so that she could face him. "What did you say?"

"Come with me," she blurted out. "Build a new life, a future with me." She had thought about it long and hard. Every moment over the years had Frederick in it, well, her happy ones, that is. He was more than her closest friend.

He was her heart.

Frederick arched a brow, a slight grin on his lips. "Are you saying that you might love me, Miss Gordon?"

"Yes," she breathed. "I believe I do."

"Well, then," he said after a moment, reaching into the pocket of his coat. "Then perhaps we better make this official, before we take off to Gretna Green."

Della gasped as she saw the small gold ring he held in his fingertips, the sunlight glinting off the metal. "Marry me," Frederick stated, his expression tender. "Be my wife."

"Yes," Della exclaimed, watching as he slid the ring onto her finger. Unlike last time, she felt hope, happiness, and more importantly, she felt love.

EPILOGUE

TWO YEARS LATER

"*A*re you certain this is where you want it? My dear, you've made me move this chair five times in the last hour."

Della smirked as she watched her father slide the chair back to the place that he had pushed it from originally, seeing Charlotte's frown as he did so. "No, I don't like it there," she admonished. "The sun will be in my eyes."

Thomas Gordon sighed, dropping into the chair himself. "Well, then, you will have to shade them."

Charlotte glared at him, and Della chose that moment to escape to the garden outside the study. The air was crisp, but the sun was warm, and she tilted her face toward the sky, breathing in the smell of the fragrant flowers that were blooming. It was days like this that Della could count her many blessings that had been bestowed on her and her family, after all that she had endured in her lifetime.

Never again would her family have to suffer. They had more funds than they knew what to do with in a lifetime. The manor was large enough to house those that were closest to her and the rolling lands below them offered a sense of peace that they would never find in the city. When they had first arrived, she thought that it would be too much, that they would never call it home.

Now, it was the only home she ever wished to have.

"There you are."

Della turned at the sound of her husband's voice. "I had to get out of the study before they went at it again."

Frederick slid his arms around her waist and Della leaned against him, letting him press his lips to her temple. "They care for each other. She just likes to rile him up a bit."

Della smiled. She knew that her father and Charlotte had a special relationship, having endured their time in King's Bench and coming out unscathed. "Lady Christine will be here in the morrow."

Frederick groaned. "You did it on purpose, didn't you? You know that Ron is going to be here as well."

Della's smile grew. She wouldn't admit it to her husband, but she might have done it on purpose. The older woman had truly become a close friend to Della since that day in London, and she always looked forward to her visits. Ron, on the other hand, seemed to be afraid of the woman, but not frightened enough to steal looks at dinner when they were all together. "He will be fine."

"He will detest you!" Frederick chuckled, tightening his hold on her.

Della sighed as she watched the day pass around them. Never did she think she could be as happy as she was now, but it was all because of her husband, her family, this place. Everything she could have hoped for was all around her.

"You truly should go in and rescue your father," her husband said after a moment.

"I know," she replied, turning in his arms. "But I would like to spend more time with you instead."

Frederick pressed his forehead to hers, drawing in a breath. "Well, now, I might be inclined to let him suffer a bit longer for the presence of my wife's company."

Della laid her hand on his chest, feeling the beat of his heart under the linen of his shirt. "Frederick, I must tell you something."

"All right," he said softly. "You know you can tell me anything."

"I'm going to get bigger," she blurted out.

He stepped back, his eyes wide and Della gave him a little smile. When she had found out that she was carrying his child, her first thoughts were of elation. This babe was a product of their love for each other.

Then her thoughts had turned to her mother and how Della would have enjoyed telling her of her coming grandchild. However, if her father had never been sent to King's Bench, Della would have never met the love of her life or the people that she now considered family.

"Della," he breathed, wiping a hand over his face. "Are you certain?"

She nodded, placing a hand on her stomach. "Yes."

He let out a shout and grabbed her by the waist, spinning her around in a slow circle. Della laughed as he did so. "Frederick!"

"Oh Della," he said, gathering her close. "You have made me so very happy."

She embraced him tightly, tears sparkling in her eyes. "You make me happy, my love."

He pulled back, clearing his throat. Della was surprised to see the glimmer of tears in his eyes as well. "We should tell the others."

"In a moment," Della said, gathering him close once more. "I want to enjoy the silence a little while longer." Having this babe would change their lives but it would be for the better. Generations from now, their grandchildren and great grandchildren would stand in this exact spot and hopefully see the beauty of Scotland, of the love that was planted here in their love and those after them.

And then, when their bones turned to dust, perhaps there would be a tale about a girl who had survived, one that had given everything she had for those that she loved and was rewarded in the end with happiness beyond measure...

~*~*~

Thank you so much for reading my story.

If you enjoyed reading this book may I suggest that you might also like to read my recent release 'Emma's Forlorn Hope' next which is available on Amazon for just £0.99 or free with Kindle Unlimited.

Click Here to Get Your Copy Today!

Sample of First Chapter

Rain fell hard against the windowpanes, the thick splatters sounding like gunshots in the quiet and dark of the house. Though it was day, the ashen grey clouds blanketed the world like a death shroud. There was a chill in the air, a driving wind clawing its way through the cracks in the stonework and whistling like angered banshees through the house. The raging elements made it hard to think and Emma Moss could not have been more thankful for it. Thinking was the last thing she wanted, as was silence. For the last two days, the house had been quiet as the grave and she could hardly stand it. Angry though the elements were, their raging cacophony was welcome to the nothingness that had taken over her home.

Sat in the rocking chair at her mother's bedside, Emma stared blankly at the windows, watching them rattle whilst trying to count each raindrop. Dark rings circled her eyes and her cheeks were stained with the dried-up channels of tears that no longer flowed. Wrapped in an old, frayed shawl, Emma barely noticed the cold. She was far too numb.

By her side, Emma's mother lay silent and quiet in the bed, covered in as many layers of blankets as Emma could find about the house. She would have had a fire going, except water had gotten to the logs. She hadn't bothered to complain to Father. Since Mother had fallen ill, the man had come undone. Though never very reliable to begin with, Thomas Moss was nothing without his wife. He was a boat and she the rudder. Emma was told it had always been so, and that her father would never have amounted to anything in life without her mother's influence. Now, as the woman they both loved lay silent and dying in her bed, Emma felt she truly understood the kind of man her father was. Content to wallow in ennui and self-pity, he had holed himself away in the quiet corners of the house for the past days, never once looking to cook for or check after his children. Emma had to ride out to the wet nurse in the nearby village to beg her care for her young sister for a few days, and she was glad she had done so. If left under her father's watch, Emma was certain baby Mary would have been left to starve.

As dissatisfied thoughts of her father swirled through her head, Emma let out a sigh. She tried to ignore the dark and empty fireplace and instead thought about slipping beneath the covers of her mother's bed. Their combined warmth would do them both good, she thought.

With nothing to be done until dinner and the doctor's next visit, Emma made up her mind. Rising up from the chair, the floor creaked loudly underfoot as she moved around the bed and slipped beneath the patchwork covers. She had hoped she was quiet enough not to disturb her mother's rest, but she felt a stirring beneath the sheets as she lay down next to the woman who had raised and nurtured her.

"Thomas... Is that you? Finally risked coming back to your own bed?"

"No, Mama, it's me," Emma spoke softly. She heaved a sigh as she turned her head into the pillows. She wanted to apologise for her father never being there, but it was not her crime to apologise for.

"Your father still sitting in the living room? If he's not careful he'll run out of chances to see me," Mrs Moss said, her voice a pitiful whisper.

"Don't speak like that Mother," Emma said, pushing in a little closer and wrapping her arms around the woman who had raised her.

"Where's Mary?" Mrs Moss asked, before descending into a fit of coughing. Emma sat up and passed over a pewter cup of water. Her mother swallowed a few grateful sips then coughed again.

As Emma took back the glass, she could not help but notice the flecks of blood on the rim of the cup. "Where's Mary?" the woman asked again.

"I told you last time you woke, I sent her to Elsie Brown, the wet nurse. She's promised to look after Mary at no charge until you get better."

"Does she know that'll mean adopting her?" Mrs Moss asked, her gallows humour earning no laugh from her daughter.

The room fell to silence once more, mother and daughter both lying wrapped up together and listening to the sound of the driving rain. Emma held her mother tight in her arms, possessively.

"You know you can't afford to be like your father," Emma heard her mother say, her voice softer.

"Mother?"

"You can't keep going through life finding ways to pretend everything is fine when the house is burning down around you."

"I don't think there is any chance of that with all this rain," Emma joked, trying desperately to deflect her mother's message.

"You know what I mean, Emma," her mother said. She turned now, staring into her eldest daughter's eyes. It was the most alert and together she had seemed in days and yet Emma felt a shudder pass through her as she studied her mother's face. It was so sallow, her skin like paper hanging off her bones. Her hair was limp and lifeless, and she just seemed exhausted—thoroughly and completely. "I want to know that you will look after Mary," the woman continued. There was an edge to her voice, her request one that Emma could not dismiss or bat aside with empty assurances.

"Will you look after Mary when I am gone, Emma?" her mother asked again. Beneath the sheets, her hands moved to find her daughter's, winding their fingers together and grasping tight. "I need to know that you won't abandon her or let anything bad happen to her. I... I love your father, but I know what he is like, too. He won't be any good at all when I'm gone. I need to know I can rely on you to look after yourself and your sister."

Emma bit her bottom lip. She thought she was done with crying. In the last days she had shed so many tears she felt certain she had nothing left to give. Still, as she tried to summon up the words to answer her mother, she felt the familiar dampness on her cheeks, the hateful blurring at the edges of her vision. She couldn't refuse to answer her mother, at the same time she wanted so desperately to ignore the question. Emma couldn't explain it, but she felt at that moment as if she had the power over life and death with her answer. It felt like her mother was asking for her permission to die, ready to slip away once Emma gave her the assurance that she needed to enter that last and deepest of rests.

"Mother, I..."

"Please, Emma," the woman begged again, her dull eyes staring intently at her.

"You know I won't let anything happen to Mary," Emma said at last. The words were halting, broken between half sobs as she nestled into her mother and rested her head in the crook of her neck.

"That's my good girl," came a voice that seemed eerily peaceful and distant. Emma took deep lungfuls of air as she tried to calm herself. No further words passed between them. Emma did not know what else to say, only able to communicate her feelings by the way she held fast to her mother in the dark.

Her eyes flickered open. Outside, the rain had eased to a dull drizzle and the wind calmed to a respectful whisper. It was later than Emma had expected it to be. The bedroom was swathed in darkness and there was no light from under the door frame. The dark clouds of day had drawn into a night, black as pitch, and Emma could hardly even make out her mother's form in the bed. Even without sight, Emma felt something was wrong.

Her mother was still, her body limp in a way that didn't feel like sleep. Emma's hand ran down her mother's arm, moving to her wrist to check for a pulse. For a moment, Emma's whole body tensed, and her lips pursed with worry. Her eyes stared into the dark ahead of her, unfocused and empty as she confirmed her suspicions.

Although there had been weeks to prepare and days to contemplate the possibility of her mother's death, Emma had put it off. Lying next to the unmoving and silent body, she felt as if she should feel something. She should start to cry again, wrap her arms about her mother and hold her as grief took over. Those felt like the right and natural things to do, but Emma found no compulsion or desire to do either.

Instead, she sat up. Sat up and pulled herself out of bed, taking a moment to light the nearby candle on the bedside table. In the faint illumination, she busied herself. She straightened the bed sheets and turned her mother so that she lay flat on her back with hands clasped together over her chest. This done, Emma found her shoes and slipped them on.

Stepping out into the hall, the girl found no light shining anywhere in the house. She held the candle in her hand firmly as she walked through to the living area and kitchen. There was a weak two-day-old broth in one of the pans left for them to eat. It was not much, but it would do until she could go out to the town in the morning. Finding the last of the coal in the kitchen, Emma set about lighting the stove, making a mental note of all that would need doing the next day.

There was the undertaker to inform and the parish priest. Doctor Philips would also need to know, and as Emma thought of the man, she wondered why he had not called as agreed. It did not matter much she told herself, focussing on what food she would need to purchase. How long could she leave Mary in the care of Mrs Brown? She had no doubt the kindly wet nurse would agree to look after her baby sister as long as was needed, but Emma couldn't take advantage of that generosity. Besides, she had promised mother that she would see to Mary.

The ongoing list of duties, responsibilities and plans marched on through Emma's mind as she stirred up the old broth in the pan. She stared into the liquid, hardly noticing as a shadow moved behind her. Only when the corner chair creaked did she realise her father had walked in. No doubt he could smell the food.

"How is she?" came the tentative question.

Emma almost didn't want to answer. She wasn't looking to spare her father's feelings or avoid the topic. Instead, she felt as though he had no right to know what had happened. He had chosen to lock himself away the last days and nights, resolutely shuttering the world out to wallow in self-pity. He didn't deserve to know anything. If he wanted to know he should march into his bedroom and see for himself.

"She's dead," Emma answered simply, knowing it would do no good to indulge in petty revenge. She stopped stirring the broth in the pan for a moment, listening for any sign of life or emotion behind her.

She did not turn around though, not wishing to look her father in the eyes.

"Was it quick?" The man's voice was weak when he spoke, but Emma heard it.

"I don't know. I know she had fallen asleep. I closed my eyes to rest and when I woke again, she was gone." There was no emotion in her voice, just facts; as if she was telling the news of someone wholly unrelated to her.

For a few minutes, all was silent. Father said nothing, and Emma could not hear him stirring from his chair behind her. She continued with the cooking, stirring the remaining soup until it was bubbling hot. She then dished the meagre meal into two bowls and carried them over to the table. One she lay down before her father, not even looking him in the eyes as she did so. The other, she took to her own place.

"I'll need to see several people in town tomorrow," Emma said, her voice wooden and mechanical. "You'll need to see about going back to work soon. I can't look after Mary and go out to wash and clean for the Parr family."

"We'll move to the city," Thomas said, his voice matter of fact and strangely resolute. He too seemed numbed by everything, left empty and emotionless.

"The city?" Emma sucked in a breath, feeling a twinge of uncertainty. "Why would you say that?"

"It's where the work is," Thomas replied. "I can't expect to get anything here, not after what happened around the time your mother fell ill. Besides, I don't much feel like staying on in this place."

Emma took a sip of soup between pursed lips. "Do you know what you'd do in London?" she asked, trying to put on that voice her mother used to keep a check on him.

"I'll find something," he said, following the words up with a too-casual shrug.

And that was the end of it. Both numb, both unwilling or unable to grieve as they should, father and daughter ate their meal in silence, with the prospect of a new start in the city added to Emma's fears and uncertainties for the future...

~*~*~

This wonderful Victorian Romance story —
'Emma's Forlorn Hope' — is available on Amazon
for just £0.99 or *FREE* with Kindle Unlimited
simply by clicking on the link below.

Click Here to Get Your Copy of 'Emma's Forlorn Hope' - Today!

A NOTE FROM THE AUTHOR

Dear Reader,

Thank you so much for choosing and reading my story — I sincerely hope it lived up to your expectations and that you enjoyed it as much as I loved writing about the Victorian era.

This age was a time of great industrial expansion with new inventions and advancements.

However, it is true to say that there was a distinct disparity amongst the population at that time — one that I like to emphasise, allowing the characters in my stories to have the chance to grow and change their lives for the better.

Best Wishes
Ella Cornish

Newsletter

If you love reading Victorian Romance stories…

**Simply sign up here and get your FREE copy of
The Orphan's Despair**

Click Here to Download Your Copy - Today!

More Stories from Ella!

If you enjoyed reading this story you can find more great reads from Ella on Amazon…

Click Here for More Stories from Ella Cornish

Contact Me

If you'd simply like to drop us a line you can contact us at **ellacornishauthor@gmail.com**

You can also connect with me on my Facebook Page **https://www.facebook.com/ellacornishauthor/**

I will always let you know about new releases on my Facebook page, so it is worth liking that if you get the chance.

LIKE Ella's Facebook Page **_HERE_**

I welcome your thoughts and would love to hear from you!

Printed in Great Britain
by Amazon

69665334R00108